SEX AND LOATHING IN HOLLYWOOD

First Edition

Published by The Nazca Plains Corporation
Las Vegas, Nevada
2008

ISBN: 978-1-934625-61-3

Published by

The Nazca Plains Corporation ®
4640 Paradise Rd, Suite 141
Las Vegas NV 89109-8000

PUBLISHER'S NOTE
Sex and Loathing in Hollywood is a work of fiction created wholly
by *Tim Desmondes'* imagination. All characters are fictional and any
resemblance to any persons living or deceased is purely by accident. No
portion of this book reflects any real person or events.

Cover Photos, Rui Vale De Sousa and Gordon Galbraith
Art Director, Blake Stephens

DEDICATION

This book is dedicated to the denizens of Hollywood, the most fascinating village on Earth. Ever since I can remember, I have loved you and the industry you exemplify.

SEX AND LOATHING IN HOLLYWOOD

First Edition

Tim Desmondes

CONTENTS

INTRODUCTION

Hollywood is more than a neighborhood in the city of Los Angeles. It is a mythical village inhabited by the best known characters in the entire world.

Hollywood is synonymous with motion pictures and has been so from the earliest days of the industry.

None of the characters in the following pages are depictions of any one actual actor, actress, director, screenplay writer, or any other of the denizens of workers in the business.

However, the author was born and raised in Los Angeles and has had contact with enough Hollywood types to feel that he can realistically portray the imaginary characters in this book.

The characters are all fictional and do not portray any real life person, either living or dead.

PART ONE
OLD FRIENDS

CHAPTER ONE

When Henri woke up in the morning, he was flaccid. He was only thirty five years old, but was already suffering from a depleting libido. But he drew strength from the nubile body asleep next to him. He reached over to feel the youthful exuberance of his bed companion.

The firmness of his bedmate's shaft always caused Henri to grow nostalgic, recalling his salad days when he always awoke turgid.

His lover and companion was Rock Stone, an eighteen-year-old male starlet who got bit parts at Olympic Studios and an occasional moment in television commercials. A delightful and tasty young stud.

Henri's apartment, Number 322 at the Emperor's Arms Apartments in Hollywood adjoined Rock's apartment, Number 323. That was no accident since Henri paid the rent for both places. Henri could not have an actual male roommate. That could be damaging to his image as one of Hollywood's leading men – Henri Gabin, the Great French Lover.

When Henri took gentle purchase on Rock's member, Rock's eyes sprung open. Nothing will shake a man awake like having his cock grabbed, however gentle that grab may be. Even so, Rock was used to it. Most mornings he was awakened by that startling feeling of an erotic dream being punctuated by the sensation of a warm hand grazing the very core of his being.

"Good Morning, Rock."

Rock always woke up with a hardon. He also always awoke with the need to pee. So his answer to the loving touch to his mid-region and the friendly, French accented, "Good morning, Rock," was usually answered by simply removing his bedmate's hand from his dong, slipping out of bed, and mouthing something like "morning."

By the time Rock reached the bathroom, his flag had descended sufficiently to allow him to relieve himself.

He rinsed his mouth, took a swig of Listerine, gargled, and then admired his handsome young face with its overnight blond stubble in the mirror.

Now it was time to pay the rent. That is to say, to insure Henri of his morning romp. By delivering sexual satisfaction to his lover and companion, Rock had free rent and use of Apartment 323. He also got breakfast at Henri's, plus regular, but not overly-generous, infusions of cash into his often hungry wallet.

The feel of Rock's cock had caused Henri's member to sluggishly perk up. But by the time Rock returned to the bed, the tired thing had lost its enthusiasm.

Rock's first actual job of the morning was to suck Henri's tiny cock to a full erection. This always worked in a matter of seconds. Rock's mouth music was worth a pack of Viagra pills. Once Henri was ready for action, Rock was allowed the choice of what they would do. Henri was the top man and Rock the bottom. Yet the youth was allowed to decide on the morning's drill. He could take Henri further in his mouth, take him in the ass, or exercise his hand.

This morning, as indeed on most mornings, he chose mutual j.o. It was the least taxing, and always satisfied Henri's need for rejuvenation just fine.

After each man had achieved his morning orgasm, Henri went to the bathroom to brush, shower, and shave while Rock prepared breakfast for the two of them. He always did the food preparation nude because Henri got pleasure from watching that well-muscled body moving around in the kitchen as he stepped out of the bathroom.

Henri got fully dressed and sat opposite his nude male lover at the breakfast table. A half grapefruit, French toast, bacon, and coffee. The boy was such a pleasure. He did the grocery shopping, using Henri's credit card reserved for that purpose alone. He prepared a savory breakfast. And he was a reliable lover morning and evening. A real treasure.

After breakfast, Henri was off to Lacy's apartment at the Hollywood

Egyptian Tower. Lacy was his female lover, and she would be expecting him for "tea and comfort" by ten o'clock. He was not due at the studio at all that day, so he could while away the time at his mistress' to his heart's content.

When Henri left, Rock put the dishes into the dishwasher, cleaned up around the kitchen, and went through the connecting door to his own place. His own lover, Marlene Grabo, would be coming by around ten o'clock for her morning romp.

Marlene was a star. She had been a star for about as long as Henri had. They had even made a few movies together some ten years or so ago. And had a love affair at the same time. Now, like Henri, she was being offered more "character parts" than glamour roles by the studio. She was forty years old and would admit to thirty-five or so of them. Making her, in her own eyes, the same age as her old lover Henri.

Rock performed his bathroom abutions, and got dressed in one of the expensive sports outfits Marlene had bought for him.

He needed Marlene. She paid for his gym membership. She bought him the most stylish clothes available anywhere. And she often gifted him with cash. But, like Henri, she felt it in her best interest to keep Rock somewhat financially wanting and thus dependent.

She didn't mind sharing her boy-toy with Henri. Nor did Henri begrudge her relationship with his lover. Rock's condition satisfied each. And, after all, prudery had little currency in the culture of Tinsel Town.

Before he had come to Hollywood, Rock had enjoyed extensive romantic interludes. From before high school, girls had swooned over his natural blond good looks. Sex came easily to him. He developed a certain callow finesse in the act. When Marlene "discovered" him, she taught him the nuances she had learned as a movie star for more years than she cared to admit to. He knew what was expected of him when romancing a mature woman. And he got pleasure from exhibiting his erotic expertise.

Marlene entered his apartment without knocking. She had her own key to the place. They both felt it was her right.

She was stunningly attired, as befitted the glamour queen she had once been. Her body was that of a woman half her age thanks to the regimen imposed on her by her private trainer and the scalpel incisions introduced into her body by her plastic surgeons.

Rock's ever appraising eye found no fault with what he saw. She did not turn him on like girls more nearly his own age. But she *was* still a very sexy appearing creature.

Marlene's lover had two duties. He had to adore her and he had to seduce her. The adoration part consisted in telling her constantly how glamorous, how beautiful, and how irresistible she was while exploring her body avidly with hand, mouth, tongue, and genitals. She had taught him how to utter worshipful words while simultaneously tonguing her clitoris. Rock may not have been much of an actor, but he was an apt learner, a handsome young stud, and qualified for the part.

Seduction of an aging actress who is a sure thing simply required what is known as the suspension of disbelief. Rock only had to think of the girls and boys his own age who did sometimes require seduction techniques and put the face and body of one of his recent conquests on Marlene. This kind of fantasy loving is not uncommon among even those mortals who do not dwell within Hollywood's portals.

Marlene made sure that Rock's apartment was always well-stocked with Veuve Clicquot champagne, her favorite. He always kept a couple of bottles pre-chilled.

"You are looking particularly lovely this morning, Marlene. May I offer you a glass of champagne?"

"It is rather early in the day," she replied. "But I am a trifle thirsty. I might enjoy a sip of water."

"The tap water here in Hollywood is ghastly," he replied. "I happen to have a bit of French bubbly here in this ice bucket. It is really quite pleasant and I find it preferable to the local water."

The routine varied from time to time, of course. But Rock always managed to get Marlene to assuage her thirst with one or two bottles of Madame Clicquot's sparkling grape juice while he showered her with compliments and attestations of his undying love.

Somehow, against her protestations of innocence, he always managed to get her disrobed and into the bed that dominated his bedroom. On this particular morning he had tango music ululating from the top of the line high fidelity player Marlene had installed in the room.

As his lips grazed her swan-like neck, she protested. She assured him she was not "that kind of a girl." But her moans, surprisingly in synch with the beat of the tango, suggested otherwise.

He whispered sweet nothings to her world-famous bosom. As he blew on the nub of her nipple, he watched it harden and incorporated that blooming pip into his mouth. While he was engaged in suckling he was excused from rhapsodizing orally about her charms. His mouth was silently singing paeans to the orbs that still drew the interest of a certain generation.

Next, attention was directed to that abdomen whose navel had dazzled the millions in her bare-midriffed harem-girl costumes of yore. As he mouthed around the area, with playful tongue thrusts into the bellybutton, he went through a litany of her charms. He accomplished this on auto-pilot. The lines were trite and banal, but they flowed with a logorrhea that caused the great actress' vulva to clench. Again, to the rhythm of "Jealousy," oozing from the hi-fi.

Marlene's legs and ankles were legendary. And were easy for Rock to praise. He had fucked few chicks of any age with comparable gams.

A particular technique he had developed since arriving in Hollywood was using his cock as a stimulating agent. He ran his instrument up and down her thighs, drawing designs, approaching the "Y" slowly, teasingly.

When the tip of his prick nudged the hood of her clit, her pussy began quivering in anticipation. She reached down and stroked her clit with the glorious knob that crowned his manhood.

In a shriek that resounded across to the Hollywood Hills she exclaimed, "Take me, You Mad Gorgeous Fool. I am all yours."

The mad gorgeous fool plunged his shaft into the panting vagina. Having been relieved of a load by Henri not too long before, he still was able to pleasure her with ten, eleven, twelve, thirteen thrusts before filling her with his warm, thick essence.

He got out of bed and brought her a flute of champagne while she delved into her purse for her cigarette and holder. He offered her the flute while simultaneously flicking the bedside lighter and holding it to the cigarette.

Rock did not smoke. Tobacco that is. He was never adverse to inhaling a bit of pot when with his age mates. He thought of tobacco as a pleasure for people his mother's age. He did, however, join his lover in sipping the Veuve Clicquot.

When she had finished her cigarette and champagne, they set their glasses on a bedside table and Rock stretched out for Marlene's detailed exploration of his musculature.

Rock had always been a better than average athlete. And had worked out with weights from his early teens. So he brought a well-developed set of muscles with him to Hollywood from Chicago.

Marlene paid Rip Hanks, the personal trainer at Brewster's Gym, handsomely to perfect each and every one of Rock's muscles to even more perfect display. She was paying for those youthful muscles and intended, every time she was in bed with them, to run her fingers over the merchandise.

She had paid for and bedded young musculatures for many a year. And had learned the names of the muscles and loved to articulate them as she brushed her beautifully manicured fingers over each one as it flexed and rippled for her pleasure.

She worked her way, muscle by muscle, down to the one "muscle" she truly adored.

Marlene had practiced fellatio for a good number of years. Rock had to grant that she was a pretty proficient cocksucker for a chick. Not as versatile, of course, as some of the dudes of his acquaintance. But damned good, anyway.

She released his cock from the grasp of her lips.

"I want to see you come," she insisted.

Rock had ammunition in reserve. As the jism erupted from his dick, she licked it off his abs as they tightened and quivered.

Another flute of champagne enhanced the flavor she loved, the essence of youth.

Rock told her he had a ten-thirty audition at the Pan-Global ad agency down on Sunset to try out for a laxative commercial. He elaborated that the part called for him to reach for Brand-X, while a somewhat overweight lady admonished him to choose a gentler stool softener. He laughed that if he landed the gig, the residuals would be welcome enough to make the teasing taunts of his pals bearable.

He dressed again in the classy sports outfit Marlene had provided for him. She stayed behind in the apartment to kill the opened bottle of wine.

She lounged. She smoked. She drank. She put a CD of Viennese waltzes in the player. She admired her epidermis in all three of the full-length mirrors that graced the walls.

Marlene leafed through the papers in one of her lover's dresser drawers.

A letter in progress was in a pile of papers. The dear boy was writing a letter to a person who apparently was an uncle. It began "Dear Unkie Al."

She stretched out on the bed, her upper body supported by the oversized pillows she had bought for Rock's bed.

She lit a cigarette and began to read the draft Rock had made of a letter to a dear relative. How amusing.

"Dear Unkie Al,

"You will be pleased to know I have met the girl of my dreams."

Imagine, me. The 'girl of his dreams.' What a sweetheart the laddie is.

"I have asked her to marry me, and she has blessed me by accepting my proposal."

Proposal? What kind of shit is this?

18

"I know you will approve of my choice. She is a very sweet girl, much involved in church work..."

Church work? He sure as Hell doesn't seem to be thinking of me. Proposal! Church work! That sneaky little son of a bitch. He's trying to slip out of my grasp.

"Her name is Lacy Greeland. I am enclosing a picture of her so you can see the sweet innocent face that has captured my heart."

Christ almighty. Lacy! That whore! Picture?

Marlene ransacked the papers in the dresser drawer. But there was no picture of Lacy.

"That son of a bitch bastard I've been helping out. And he's going to get married to Lacy, one of Hollywood's most notorious courtesans. A woman who was one of my lovers back...a while ago. This calls for action!"

Lacy Greeland's telephone number was not listed in the Hollywood phone book. But Marlene's network of sources soon enough provided a telephone number and an address Marlene recognized. Lacy was living at the Hollywood Egyptian Tower Apartments on Cahuenga.

"Hello, Lacy Dear? Guess who's calling? I knew you'd recognize my voice immediately. Everyone does. But, especially old dear friends like you. It's been ages, hasn't it? And I've missed seeing you so. Look, Darling. I just *must* see you. It's an emergency. Life or death matter you know. Would you be an angel and spare a few minutes for me this morning? Oh, no! It can't wait. You're at the Hollywood Egyptian Tower, aren't you? I'll be right there, Dear. Ta-ta!"

Marlene was out of the Emperor's Arms as fast as she could get herself dressed and into her Bentley.

CHAPTER TWO

Marlene Grabo and Lacy Greeland's relationship went back ten years. Back then they were bosom friends. They were in two movies together, *Slave Girls of the Harem*, and *The Garden of Ali*. Marlene, of course, played Yasmin, the harem girl who became Princess of Qatar. Her co-star was Henri Gabin, who played Prince Ali. Lacy was one of the pretty faces among the anonymous harem girls.

Marlene found Lacy attractive and invited her to her dressing room. The two enjoyed the same love-play, and became devote lovers. Lacy naively believed a romantic liaison with the famous actress might further her own career. She later woke up to Hollywood reality and realized that none of Marlene Grabo's many lovers, male or female, ever advanced as much as a millimeter in the craft as a result of help from the Star.

During the period of nearly two years that Marlene and Lacy reveled in the couch of Sappho, the Star was also balling Henri, the leading man. But Lacy was not absolutely true to her partner either. She was entertaining an assistant director by the name of David Moore, who took good care of her when her movie career went down the drain.

Marlene went on to new roles and new lovers. Lacy went on to new directors, producers, writers, cameramen and actors. She lived a full, happy life as mistress to some of Hollywood's so-called nobility.

Marlene was in her Bentley, Hell-bent to confront her old bosom buddy. She was not ready to jettison Rock Stone yet. She loved 'em young, hard, broke, and dependent.

As a matter of fact, Henri loved Rock for pretty much the same reasons.

Marlene had no idea who this "Unkie Al" was.

Unkie Al was not Rock's uncle at all. He liked to be called Unkie Al by the young people he knew. He was, indeed, of an avuncular nature. He was outgoing, generous, and affectionate. He was also immensely wealthy.

Albert Pughworthy was a mining engineer by training and experience. He had discovered a copper load in Madrazo, Arizona, had purchased the land and formed a company. He became owner and CEO of the largest open pit copper mine in the world.

He had married twice, was widowed once and divorced once. The divorce was amicable enough. A dancer named Kinki from California had moved on with a generous settlement. Unkie Al thought she had been worth every million.

He had no children by either marriage. Which was not to say he did not father any children.

Some eighteen years previous, he had a memorable affair with a chorus girl named Trixie Masters. He was in Chicago on business and extended his stay, beguiled by the attractive, vivacious dancer. Unkie Al always had a soft spot in his heart for dancers. And Trixie showed him one Hell of a time.

Trixie discovered that she was with child. Unkie Al was back in Arizona when she made the discovery. When he got the word, he called his attorney and sent the legal eagle to Chicago to talk to the young lady.

Unkie did not want to get married. And he did not want to be dragged into a paternity suit. But he was willing to be very generous.

There was nothing grasping abut Trixie. She was adamantly opposed to an abortion, no matter what kind of money she might receive from the alleged father for doing so. She *would* have the baby.

Fine. Then in order for her not to name Albert Pughworthy as the father, would a gift of one million dollars be sufficient? Trixie, as already noted, was not grasping. But she consulted an attorney of her own who told her not to speak further with the rich man's lawyer. He would speak for her.

The result of the negotiations was that Trixie Masters would receive two hundred fifty thousand dollars per year for eight years as salary from the

Madrazo Copper Mining Company for her job as Chicago representative of said company. (For which she was required to do absolutely nothing at all.) It was agreed that Albert would never acknowledge the child as his own. The salary paid to Trixie in no way constituted Mr. Pughworthy's admission of paternity.

Furthermore, it was agreed that Albert Pughworthy would set up a trust for Miss Masters' child, for two million dollars, to be handed over, in bulk, to that child at age nineteen, provided he or she was married at that time. Unkie Al was not particularly homophobic. But if the recipient of the trust was male, he could not see his money going to support the gay life style. If the young man was married, that would prove he was straight. (Wouldn't it?) If Trixie gave birth to a girl, and if that girl was married before receiving the money, that would protect her from fortune hunters. (Wouldn't it?)

Trixie gave birth to a healthy boy, Albert Masters by name, no father's name on his birth certificate.

Little Albert had a happy enough childhood to the age of twelve. He was surrounded by luxury, and by a series of putative uncles. Unfortunately, his mother had squandered the entire salary she had received from Madrazo, and died with a smile on her face when her son was twelve years old.

His grandmother raised him through his teens, and sent him off to Hollywood with her blessing when he turned eighteen, having helped him to change his name legally to Rock Stone.

Unkie Al had kept in touch with his "nephew" watching his career in Hollywood from afar at Chupapollo Ranch, in Madrazo, Arizona.

CHAPTER THREE

Lacy knew there was no way to fend off her old friend's imminent visit. Henri was napping in the bedroom and she decided not to awaken him for the visit. He was unlikely to relish a conversation with Marlene Grabo. Let him sleep off the rather tepid sexual encounter of a half-hour ago.

The doorbell rang. Lacy opened it. There was a succession of oohs and aahs, of pecks at cheeks with pursed lips and insincere hugs.

"Marlene, Darling. It *has* been ages. Do come in and make yourself comfortable."

Marlene answered with, "How lovely you look, Lacy Dear."

She stepped into the apartment and looked around. She was satisfied that the place had been tastelessly decorated.

"What stunning décor," she sniffed. "You *must* give me the name of your decorator."

Lacy felt no need to respond to the statement.

"You look as ravishing as ever, my dear Marlene. Won't you sit down?"

As Marlene settled herself gracefully on the sofa she enthused, "My, what a gorgeous idea. You were always so clever, Lacy."

Lacy made Marlene an offer she knew she couldn't refuse.

"May I offer you a drink?"

Marlene consulted her watch.

"My word! Eleven o'clock in the morning. Why yes. Perhaps a little eye opener."

There was a wet bar with refrigerator in a corner of the room.

"I just happen to have a bottle of gin in the freezer department," she offered.

"Sapphire?"

"What else?"

The ladies had always shared a penchant for the same gin.

"I would be delighted, Darling."

Lacy took a bottle of gin, two frosted Martini glasses, and a jar of cocktail olives out of the refrigerator and placed them on the coffee table along with two coasters and napkins.

"It's been so long, Dear. Would you care for one olive or two?" Lacy asked.

"Oh, none, Darling. The damned things displace too much gin, don't they?"

Lacy smiled conspiratorially and put the olives back in the refrigerator. Marlene had always been so right about so many things.

Lacy poured the gin into the glasses, sat next to Marlene on the sofa and the two ladies clicked their glasses.

"Kismet," they said in unison. It was the toast from their days with each other at the studio.

"Those were the days, weren't they?" Lacy said with a certain trace of nostalgia.

"Yes," Marlene agreed. "Those two pictures we were in made scads of money for the studio."

"And for you, too, as the star."

"I suppose so," Marlene shrugged. "You know I am in the craft only for the sake of art. Not for the money."

Lacy choked on her drink.

"Ours was quite an affair, wasn't it, Marlene?"

"One of my very best, Love. With either a woman or a man."

Lacy had to ask. "I've always wondered, Darling. Was I a better lover than Rex?"

"Rex?" Marlene questioned. "Oh, yes. Rex the Wonder Dog. He was just a passing fancy. I am not kinky, you know."

"Besides," Lacy added. "I understand Rex wasn't very faithful to you."

Marlene had to admit that Rex was after every bitch in Hollywood.

The two ladies had downed their cocktails already. Lacy replenished the glasses.

Lacy felt it was time to cut the crap and cut to the chase.

"When you telephoned just now, you said you just *had* to see me right away."

Marlene was ready to get down to brass tacks, but first wanted to alert Lacy that the cocktail glasses were empty. She lifted her empty glass and made it quite clear that it was devoid of the Sapphire. Lacy had been ready to pour anyway, smiled at her guest, filled the glasses, and prepared to listen.

"It was so kind of you, Darling, to take time out of your busy morning to make room for me," Marlene cooed. "I just *had* to see you. I am devastated, Lacy. Simply devastated."

Lacy draped an arm over the shoulders of her dear, dear old friend.

"Tell your little Lacy all, Dear."

"I don't know how acquainted you are with Rock Stone..." Marlene queried.

"I'm quite aware of him. He *is* Henri's companion and lover."

"And Henri...?" Marlene probed.

"As you of course know, I am Henri Gabin's mistress. His kept woman. His lover."

"His *other* lover," Marlene clarified. "And did you know that Rock and I are an item?"

"There have been rumors around town to that effect. You always did like them young and buff."

"Who doesn't?" Marlene asked. "Henri's tastes run in that direction, too. At least with respect to studs. I'm sure you would like Rock yourself, Dear. He's all of eighteen. But he is gifted with the stamina and endurance of a fourteen-year-old."

"Right down your alley," Lacy smiled.

"I couldn't have said it better," Marlene riposted.

"I'm of course delighted you dropped by for a little morning chat about Henri or Rock. Tell me, Darling. Which of the two did you come to gossip about?"

"Do you have to ask? About Rock, of course. I visited him at his apartment this morning."

"That would be number three twenty-three at the Emperor's Arms."

"Yes. The unit connecting to Henri's apartment. It's all so discrete, isn't it? Protects the two darlings from malicious gossip."

"Gossip? In Hollywood? My dear!" Lacy joked. "Anyway, there you were this morning, at Rock's pad. Checking on his...?"

"Stamina, My Dear."

"And how did you find his...stamina?"

"Oh, my darling girl. Need you ask? How long has it been since you've had a studly eighteen-year-old?"

"Ages, Dear. Just ages," Lacy admitted with a sigh.

"After Rock and I had discussed the topics of the day, the dear boy had to rush off. He's auditioning for a part this morning."

"In the movies?"

"For a commercial. A dreary bit about some laxative."

"I suppose they're looking for someone whose ass would look good on television?"

"If so, Rock's a shoo-in for the part. He does have the cutest ass. You should see it some time. Come to think of it, that's one of the reasons for my visit other than a social occasion to see you, of course. There's nothing like old friends, is there?"

"The reason for your visit, other than purely social, is to discuss Rock Stone's ass?" Lacy asked, greatly surprised.

"As a matter of fact, yes," Marlene continued. "I was just getting to that."

"Pray proceed, Darling," Lacy said with great interest. "I'm all ears."

"Off the dear boy went for his audition."

"Sweet ass and all," Lacy added.

"Ah, yes. So I languished there in his apartment, enjoying a few moments of solitude. I take such a personal interest in everything about him that I rummaged through some personal papers of his that he had squirreled way in a dresser drawer."

"Our prerogative with our lovers," Lacy agreed.

"And among his papers, I found something shocking."

"Possibly something that caused you to think of telephoning an old, dear friend," Lacy guessed.

"Yes. I had been thinking of calling you so often, anyway, you know. I love to keep in touch with old friends."

"Aren't you sweet? Now do tell me what you found in that dresser drawer."

"A letter he was composing to his Uncle Al."

"Uncle Al?"

"Yes. There was an envelope addressed to Albert Pughworthy in that drawer. And the letter draft began with 'Dear Unkie Al.'"

"Albert Pughworthy the copper magnate?" Lacy asked. "Rock is related to the multi-millionaire Albert Pughworthy?"

"So it would seem. The darling boy never, ever mentioned to me that he had a rich relative. You know, he seldom seems to have a nickel to his name."

"A condition beneficial to you, of course."

"And to Henri as well, Dear. Our playthings have to be kept on a tight leash. We've seen what happens to them when they get too independent."

"The ungrateful louses," Lacy agreed. "I suppose Rock was hitting up his uncle for a loan."

"Oh, no, Dear. Worse than that. Much worse than that."

"What then? Give, Marlene. What was in the goddam letter?"

"In his letter he was telling his uncle he's getting married."

"To *you*? Lacy gasped.

"Don't be ridiculous, Lacy. Of course not to *me*. That would be bizarre indeed."

To someone else, then," Lacy commiserated. "You must be devastated."

"I am. Indeed I am. I am not ready to lose the dear by to marriage yet. He is just so...so satisfying to me."

"Tell me, Love. Just who did your Rock...and, of course Henri's Rock, say in this letter that he is going to marry?"

"You!" Marlene emoted, in her most dramatic tone.

Lacy burst out laughing.

"Me?" she hooted. "You jest, Dear."

"Word of honor."

"I need a drink," Lacy guffawed, refilling both their glasses. "That is really just too funny for words. There's no way ever that I would or could marry Rock Stone. An eighteen-year-old male starlet? Even if he may happen to have a rich uncle. Not in a million years. Listen. Henri is in the bedroom there. If he's asleep he has to wake up to get a load of this."

Lacy went to the bedroom door and opened it a crack.

"Henri, Dear! Are you awake?"

Henri coughed, then answered.

"Yes, Lacy. I'm just coming to. You want to come in and finish the little romp we were having?"

"Not now, Sweetheart. Come out here into the livingroom. We have a guest."

"I can't come out right away. I'm not dressed."

Lacy shrugged that off. "No matter, Henri. It doesn't make any difference. It's only old Marlene."

Marlene was not particularly pleased by being referred to as "only old Marlene." But it was not the time or place to make an issue of it.

"Marlene Grabo?" Henri asked.

"Of course Marlene Grabo. She's seen you undressed often enough. You won't shock her. There's no room for false modesty or prudery in this place."

"Okay, if you say so."

Henri stepped into the livingroom stark naked.

"Hello, Marlene," he said graciously, in his best French accent. "Nice of you to drop by. How have you been?"

Marlene had not seen Henri nude for years. She looked him over and decided he had not improved since last time. He still had the smallest prick of anyone who had ever pleasured her (with the possible exception of Rex).

"Hello, Henri. You're looking splendid."

She would have loved to run her hand around his balls to see how that squirt of a dong would respond after all these year. But there *is* such a thing as propriety.

Henri saw the martini glasses out.

"I see you two are enjoying a bit of brunch. May I join you?"

No one answered the rhetorical question. Henri was already over at the refrigerator extricating a bottle of rum, some daiquiri mix and a tray of ice cubes. He mixed himself a daiquiri.

He held his drink out to the ladies, took a swig, and sat down on an overstuffed chair facing his mistress and the surprise guest.

"You can't imagine what Marlene came by to tell us, Dear," Lacy said.

"I'm sure it was not to tell us she's given up gin," he answered.

"No," Lacy laughed. "But something nearly as unlikely."

Henri took a long swallow of his cool drink and raised an eyebrow.

"Tell me," he requested.

"She says I'm gong to marry Rock."

"My Rock? Or rather our Rock?" Henri asked. "Rock Stone?"

He burst out laughing.

"Marlene, Marlene!" He guffawed. "That is the damnedest thing I ever heard. Whatever led you to that crazy idea?"

Marlene did not like being scoffed at. Particularly by an ex-lover sitting before her buck-ass naked.

She replied, "I happen to know he is writing a letter to a certain Unkie Al, who apparently is Albert Pughworthy the wealthy..."

She didn't get through her sentence. Henri burst out laughing anew.

"Speak no further, Marlene. I understand the situation completely. You are aware that Rock is in a parlous condition financially."

"Of course. Neither you nor I keep him flush with cash."

"Naturally. Giving money to children is hardly our thing, is it? But he has incurred a few debts that are causing him some embarrassment."

"I have been aware of that," Marlene said. "He's becoming embarrassingly insistent on gifts of money recently. I, of course, told him 'we'll see.'"

"Meaning not in a million years."

"Of course."

"You and I are still alike in so many ways," Henri said. "Dear Rock and I have probably had identical conversations to the ones you have had with him concerning money."

"So where does this uncle person fit in?" Marlene asked. "Rock's uncle can get him out of his financial dilemma. So you and I might find the dear boy's...services...somewhat curtailed in the future. That's fair enough. Although I would never help him and thus lose what control I have over him, I would never stand in his way of finding financial assistance of his own. After all, there are always plenty of young men in Hollywood for the likes of us. Aren't there?"

Marlene had to agree.

Marlene asked, "But then, what's this about him marrying dear, dear Lacy?"

"Rock has not let it be generally known. But once, when he was deep in his cups, he told me his rich uncle has set up a trust for him. What the lurid details are I don't know. But the upshot is that the dear boy will receive a couple of million dollars on his nineteenth birthday."

"How perfectly ghastly," Marlene gasped. "And where does our Lacy fit into this?"

"Rock receives the money on the condition that he is married. Something about a proof that he's straight, I think. Anyway, our boy is pulling a scam on this uncle. He has to pretend to be married to get the money. He has to provide a name of the prospective bride. He obviously cannot name you. So he apparently wrote the old man that he's marrying Lacy."

The situation amused Marlene."

"That *is* rich," she laughed. "Rock is telling his uncle he's marrying a whore."

Lacy did not take umbrage.

"Marlene, Dear," she said. "All of us who are or have been in the business are whores of one kind or another. I qualify myself as a courtesan. You are a different kind of whore. But a whore nonetheless."

Henri nodded his head, aware that he, too, was as much a whore as either of them.

Marlene continued on as chipper as could be.

"Lacy, Dear. I meant nothing personal in my remark. Let's not get nasty. It *is* just too amusing for words, though, Isn't it?"

Henri summed up the situation.

"You have nothing to worry about, Marlene. Rock will pull his scam. We won't have as much control over him any more, but he will probably continue to keep your bed warm. His relative independence may make him more difficult to manage. But I feel you may actually enjoy the challenge."

"I'm so relieved," she said. I certainly would not wish to stand in the delightful lad's way of resolving his financial situation. So, now, to change the subject. What's this I hear about you going legit? Everyone is talking about it, you know."

"Yes," Henri agreed. "It is true. My agent called to tell me they've made a stage play from the script of The Mad Lover of Notre-Dame. And, naturally, they want me to play the lead role on Broadway."

"How exciting," Marlene enthused. "When are you leaving for New York?"

"Early tomorrow morning," Henri replied.

"Well, it has been delightful," Marlene said. "But I must be on my way. Just wonderful to see you two. I'm so *very* fond of you both."

"Yes," Marlene agreed. "We really are all intimately acquainted, aren't we?"

The door bell rang. Lacy went to answer.

"Rock," she exclaimed. "Come in. Henri isn't dressed, but we won't let that bother us. And guess who's here? Marlene."

CHAPTER FOUR

Rock stepped into the livingroom. Henri did not get out of his chair but held his glass towards Rock in greeting.

Rock was surprised to see Marlene in the room.

"Marlene! What the fuck are *you* doing here?"

"I was just leaving," Marlene answered.

"Any news about your audition?" Henri asked.

"Yeah. That's what I dropped by to tell you. I think I did real good. They'll let me know for sure next week.

"Splendid," Henri said.

Lacy couldn't let a moment of mischief pass by.

"Oh, Rock," she said. "Before Marlene leaves. Wouldn't this be a marvelous time to tell us about your upcoming marriage."

Rock stammered.

"My...marriage?"

Henri stood up and pointed to a chair.

"Yes, Dear Boy. Why don't you clear things up for our friend Marlene?"

Poor Rock was flummoxed. Not only was he caught having to explain his scam. He was too new to Tinsel Town to be comfortable talking to his two lovers and benefactors at the same time. Especially when one of them was standing openly in front of everyone with his dick hanging out.

"I'll bet you could use a drink," Lacy offered.

"You got that right," Rock agreed.

"Martini or daiquiri?" she asked.

"Gin," he said, taking a seat.

Lacy brought him a nice chilled gin and everyone took a seat.

Rock downed a couple of swallows and faced up to telling his story.

Henri helped Rock by telling him he'd explained about the inheritance to the two ladies. Rock was relieved that the cat was out of the bag so he wouldn't have to try to explain the whole damned business.

Marlene admitted that she had happened to stumble onto the draft of the letter. Rock couldn't find it in him to complain about her snooping.

"That draft you saw?" he said. "I've already made a copy of it and I sent it and Lacy's picture off to Unkie Al a week ago."

To Marlene he said, "I didn't want to tell you about all this, yet, Marlene. I was going to of course. But the time never seemed right."

Everyone knew that was a lie. He hadn't meant to blab anything about the inheritance to anyone. He would surprise them with his independence when the time came. But, in a particularly dense alcoholic stupor, the story had been revealed to Henri. Up until that morning at Lacy's, Henri had seen no reason to tell anyone else his lover's secret.

"I get the money on my birthday," he went on. "So I wrote to an uncle who controls the trust, pretending I'm getting married. And, as you know I even sent him your picture, Lacy."

"How in the world?" Lacy asked.

"It's one I took at one of your parties. I had it cropped and enlarged. I didn't mean any harm."

"No problem," Lacy insisted.

Henri was encouraging.

"It's a good scam, My Boy. For your sake, I hope it works. Unkie gets the letter. He sends the dough. You're rich, pay off your debts, and are independent. Not bad at age nineteen. A happy ending to the story."

"Not quite," Rock said.

Lacy asked why not.

"Unkie is a thorough type," Rock explained. "It seems my letter wasn't enough."

"You mean he's coming here to Hollywood?" Lacy asked.

"Worse. He's already here. The truth is, he flew into Burbank this morning. I've got another kind of confession to make. That audition I told you about?"

He looked sheepishly at Marlene and Henri.

"Yes?" they answered, pretty sure of what was coming next.

"Another con job. I really went off to Burbank airport to meet Unkie."

"And?" came the question from the other three.

"He says he wants to meet the young lady. My fiancée."

"By which, I suppose, he means me?" Lacy asked.

"Which is the real reason I came by this morning," he admitted. "I have a favor to ask you, Lacy."

"I can guess what the favor is, Rock. And I sympathize with your situation. You're a nice young man. And there are a lot of things I'd be happy to do to help you. But, the answer to the question you haven't asked yet is 'no way.' I gave up acting a long time ago. And I don't do masquerades, thank you"

This sounded to Marlene and Henri like a good time to get out of the way.

"Well, Lacy Dear," Marlene said. "It has been charming to see you again. I've missed seeing you so much. We must get together more often. And now, I really must be running along."

"I understand, Darling," Lacy said. "It was so kind of you to come."

"Ta-ta, Rock," Marlene waved. "I'll see you later, I suppose."

Rock gave a half-hearted wave. "Yeah, Marlene. I'll catch up with you later."

Marlene let herself out. She was smiling. Rock and a rich uncle. A scam about marrying that whore Lacy. Delicious. She hoped the whole thing would blow up leaving Rock still wriggling under her thumb.

Henri thought it best to leave his two lovers to discuss the scam. He couldn't imagine Lacy going for it. But one can never tell, can one?

He announced, "I think I'll go get some clothes on."

"Yes Dear," Lacy agreed. "The way things are going around here, there's no telling who'll be dropping by next. We wouldn't want to be greeting guests with your lavaliere hanging out, would we?"

Henri left the room, but kept the bedroom door ajar. He had to know whether Lacy just might, by some far reach of the imagination, let herself get dragged into Rock's con.

Rock remained in the livingroom with Lacy to give his best shot at convincing her.

"Lacy, don't say 'positively no' yet. Listen to me."

"I'm listening."

"We're talking about a lot of money here."

"Go on talking," Lacy said.

"If I can pull this off, I'll come into two million dollars in just a couple of months..."

"Yes," Lacy agreed. "That is a nice chunk of money."

"And I don't need the whole two million to pay my debts and tide me over until I'm a star."

Lacy thought it might be closer to an eternity before Rock Stone was ever much more than a pretty face...and body. She didn't believe anyone saw stardom in his future. But she did not feel that her critique was particularly wanted on that subject.

"Just how much *do* you think you need?" Lacy pushed.

"I could get by nicely on a million and a half."

"Leaving five hundred thousand dollars...?" Lacy teased.

"For your help."

"Sorry, Rock," Lacy said determinedly. "Find yourself another way out. I am not going to get mixed up in this cockamamie plan for chicken feed. Henri takes good care of me. He provides me with everything I need or want. I really do not need a half a million dollars. And even if I were tempted, which I definitely am not, don't you think your uncle would consider me a bit...mature for you?"

"Golly no. He knows you're older than me. He thinks that's a good thing. It's what he calls a 'stabilizing influence.' He was actually afraid I might marry some young chick with no sense at all in her head."

"Wise Unkie," she said. "But your plan just can't work. Time is too short. Your birthday's only a couple of months away so you have to pull this off fast. Has your uncle asked yet when the wedding's going to be?"

Rock admitted he hadn't.

"What are you going to tell him when he asks?"

"Uh...I don't know. Like the wedding'll be two weeks from now?"

Lacy pointed out a flaw.

"Isn't that just dandy? Unkie says, 'Wonderful. I'll be there for the ceremony.' What do *you* say? You are aware, Rock, that there cannot be a ceremony. I wouldn't marry you for the world."

"Or me, either," Rock replied. "Imagine me marrying a..."

"A whore, Rock?"

"No. That's not what I was going to say," he gulped. "Anyway, here's the good part. Unkie is only going to be here in town until this evening. He's flying to Shanghai tonight. A big copper deal with the Chinese. Multi-million dollar contract. He'll be in China for two weeks. We'll get some pictures taken of you in a bridal gown. And maybe me in a monkey suit beside you. We'll fax those pix to Unkie in China. When he gets back, our deal's done. Unkie kisses the bride. I get the dough. Come on, Lacy. It's a sure thing. Be a pal."

"No means 'no,' Rock. There's no way I would risk anything like that for a mere five hundred thousand dollars."

Rock felt desperate. Lacy knew he was desperate. Unkie was in town and time was crucial for the kid to wrap up his deal before the old guy left. Lacy let Rock stew in his juices until he was willing to really deal.

Eventually Rock asked the question Lacy was waiting for.

"All right, Lacy. How much money would it take to get you to play fiancée and bride for a couple of months?"

"The way I see it," Lacy said. "California is a community property state. This trust money you're to get will assume you are married. By law, then, in this state, your bride is entitled to half."

Rock was flabbergasted.

"You mean you want half of everything? A whole million dollars?"

"No, Rock," she said reasonably. "It's not what I want. It's what is legally mine. If we were in some other state that doesn't have the community property law, it would be another matter. But Hollywood *is* still in California, and I would not think of breaking the law by taking less than half the magilla. So it's a million or nothing."

Rock saw Lacy's logic. He quickly concluded that a million dollars was a lot better than nothing.

Lacy, ever practical, got pen and paper and wrote up an agreement for Rock to sign. "Henri," she called into the bedroom. "Come in here, will you? I want you to witness a couple of signatures."

Henri, now fully clothed, returned to the livingroom. He knew that he might be witnessing a document that would cause him to lose a mistress and a lover. He was philosophical about it. There was no way to know whether the con would work or not. If it did, Lacy and Rock still might choose to continue their relationship with him. If not, he had never had difficulty finding a comfortable mistress and rare young meat.

Rock was now content to think of the million dollars he saw coming his way soon.

"I'm off to get Unkie," he said. "I'll be back here with him soon so he can meet my fiancée."

When Rock returned with Unkie Al, Unkie was delighted with what he saw.

He stepped into Lacy's livingroom, looked her up and down, and treated her to a strong Western hug.

"Lacy!" he enthused. "Just as pretty as your picture. Prettier. Rock can sure pick 'em."

Nice to meet you, Mr. Pughworthy," Lacy said demurely.

"No Mister Pughworthys around here, Dear. Call me Unkie Al. That's what people who like me call me."

"Would you care for a cup of coffee or anything, Unkie Al?" she asked.

"No, I can't stay around long. I've got some important business to take care of in Beverly Hills before I'm off to China. Can I use your phone? I need a taxi to pick me up here in twenty minutes or so."

Unkie Al made his call and returned to the theme of why he was there.

"I had to make time to come by and meet you. It's high time for this rascal to settle down and get married. I was concerned he'd get mixed up with some floozy and rack up a bunch of debts with fast living. I'm delighted he found a nice, simple, mature, home-girl like you. You'll knock some sense into him."

Lacy protested, politely.

"Oh, Unkie Al. I don't know about that at all. I've found Rock to be a very sensible, frugal, Christian young man. I love him as much for his morals as for his good looks and sterling character."

Unkie puffed up with pride.

"You can't imagine how glad I am to hear that, Lacy. I was worried that he might have a tendency toward wildness. He's of a wild generation. And being in Hollywood with the kind of people here. No offense."

Lacy poured it on a bit.

"Maybe our Rock was a bit wild and reckless back in Chicago. I don't know. But that was before he came to California and found Jesus."

Unkie admonished Rock.

"That's just fine, Son. But don't go getting too damned religious. You and the little lady here need to live a full life together."

"With moderation," Lacy added primly.

"Of course," Unkie agreed.

"Now, Little Lady. I happen to have brought along a little engagement present for you. I hope you'll like it."

"Oh, Unkie Al," she cooed. "How thoughtful. I just know I'll love it."

Unkie reached into his pocket and pulled out a jewel case.

"I didn't get it gift wrapped. I hope you don't mind."

When he handed the box to Lacy she was pleased to see it was from De Groton Jewelers on Rodeo Drive.

"Oh, such a pretty box," she gushed. "Shall I open it?"

"Please do," Unkie urged. "Let's see if you like it."

Lacy opened the box, and made a quick assessment of the diamond and emerald necklace inside. She knew jewelry. And she had haunted De Groton's in Beverly Hills for years. She knew this necklace had set the old boy back three grand plus.

"Put it around her neck and let's see how it looks," Unkie told Rock.

Rock got the necklace on her. She oohed and aahed and gave Unkie a hug and kiss.She told him she just *loved* it. Which, indeed, she did.

Henri walked into the room.

"Unkie," Rock said. "I'd like you to meet my friend Henri Gabin. He's Lacy's cousin and is helping me get ahead in my acting career."

Unkie shook Henri's hand enthusiastically.

"A real pleasure, Sir," Unkie said. "Rock has told me about you. His best friend. I've seen you in the movies, Mister Gabin. I'm a great admirer of your work."

Henri reciprocated.

"It is a great pleasure, Sir. Rock has told me so much about you. He admires and respects you a great deal. I was hoping to meet you."

"I believe you've been a good influence on my nephew," Unkie went on.

"I wish I could claim the honor," Henri played along. "But it is my niece, Miss Lacy, who has exerted the greatest influence on Rock's character. There is nothing like a pure woman to bring out the best in a man, is there?"

Unkie agreed, and took his leave to meet his business associate.

Lacy thanked him for the necklace, and Unkie was out the door. His taxi was waiting for him at the entrance to the building.

Lacy asked Henri and Rock if they would like something to eat. She and Henri had downed enough spirits when Marlene was there to warrant some food now in their stomachs. After his romp with Marlene earlier in the day, and with Henri still earlier, Rock had need of nourishment a well.

Lacy said she could put together some grilled cheese sandwiches and a salad. Henri and Rock accepted the idea.

Lacy went off to the kitchen to put together a bit of lunch.

Henri was happy to have a little time to discuss a concern he had with Rock.

"I have a favor to ask of you, Rock."

"Sure. Shoot!"

"You know how I feel about Lacy. You are number one in my life. But she's number two. And very dear to me."

"I know," Rock agreed. "You spend a heap of dough to keep her in this lifestyle. She's your exclusive."

"Exclusive is a good word for it, Rock. I'm going to be a continent away, and you know Hollywood."

Rock assured him he knew Hollywood but that he had no need to worry.

"I'm sure she's faithful to you, Henri."

"Of course she is," Henri agreed. "While I'm paying all the bills and am within eyesight, there's no problem. But while I'm way, she has lots of her...old acquaintances near-by. Plenty of them would just love to graze in my pasture while I'm gone."

"Gee! I see what you mean."

"There's only one person in the world I can trust to keep an eye on her, Rock. You are my best friend. And certainly my most intimate one. I trust you as if you were me. And Lacy now is going to be your pretend fiancée. So, if you take up her time, keep her away from the wolves in town, I'd feel a lot better while I'm away. I know I can trust you not to have any sexual relations with her in my absence."

"Sure, Henri. You know you can trust me. Glad to help."

"Here's a debit card I got for you, Buddy. Use it to take her out to parties, to dinner, to shows. It's backed up by two thousand dollars. And I'll put more cash behind that as needed as time goes on. Spend it freely. Show her a good time. And keep her from getting too chummy with any of her old... boyfriends."

Rock thought that sounded just great.

"You can count on me, Henri," he reiterated as he took the debit card in hand. "I'm going to miss you a lot while you're gone. Escorting Lacy around will help some. I'll stay faithful to you while you're away. You're the only guy in my life. So don't worry. There'll be no other dudes in my life while you're gone. Or chicks either."

"I'll miss you, too," Henri said. He gave Rock a deep, lingering kiss that rejuvenated his cock. So when Lacy came in with a tray full of sandwiches and a salad, she encountered two men with valiant extensions in their trousers.

Henri opened a bottle of chilled Pascal Jolivet Sancerre. Its crispness complemented the cheese sandwiches perfectly.

After lunch, Rock excused himself so his lover could bid an intimate farewell to Lacy, who was now his own fake fiancée.

He promised to be at L.A. International Airport that evening to see Henri off to New York. And, of course, to see Unkie Al off to Shanghai.

The crisp Sancerre wine seemed to make a beeline to Henri's groin. As soon as Rock was out the door, Henri and Lacy made for the bedroom.

Lacy had no difficulty urging Henri's limp cock back up to full attention. It seemed to her that she must have sucked half the troubled pricks in Hollywood to serviceable condition in her time. That skill alone accounted for probably twenty-five percent of her grateful clientele.

She was aware that in addition to the exercise of her skillful lips, Henri was lying there on the bed recalling the farewell kiss she glimpsed him bestowing on Rock. She knew the combination of her sucking and her lover's recollection of his lover was a powerful libido raiser.

Henri lay back to enjoy what he paid for. Lacy could keep a guy on the edge of ecstasy until he was delirious. Her lips, hands, feet, tits and pussy performed miracles of intimacy up and down Henri's nude, prone body. She explored not only his epidermis but the recesses of his colon. Henri was a connoisseur of the female foot, and she fondled him where he loved to be fondled with skillful footwork.

Henri's penis did not flag for a full two-and-a-half hour session of Lacy's ministrations. He was incapable of more than one ejaculation after the sessions he had had earlier that morning with her and prior to that with Rock.

Lacy knew her man. And what he needed.

That evening, Rock was at the airport. He met Unkie Al at the international terminal. Unkie slipped him an envelope stuffed with money.

"I want you to show that fiancée of yours a fine time, Son. You're only young once."

Unkie was vociferously thanked. Rock was sure he would show the little lady a time indeed with both Henri's and Unkie's money.

From the terminal he waved. "Goodbye, Unkie Al. Have a nice long stay in China."

He went on over to one of the domestic terminals. Time to wave his lover goodbye.

As he saw his lover's plane ascend into the skies his mind was weaving fantasies. He was pretty sure he would have one Hell of a time with his "fiancée while her meal ticket was out of town. Marlene would also surely continue to come to his place for her morning fuck. And there was a guy he'd noticed who had eyes for him at the gym. A real stud muffin. While Henri was away, it looked like sweet sailing.

CHAPTER FIVE

In Rock's view, the next few weeks, months, perhaps even years, should be a ball. Henri would be in New York, but paying the rent for him in Hollywood. Unkie would be in China so the road would be clear to pretend to get married and inherit a million big ones. While Henri was away, his debit card was available to live it up with Lacy.

There would be no way that Henri could find out that he was balling Lacy. And since the one restriction Henri had on the arrangement was that Lacy was to be forbidden fruit for Rock, screwing her would be even more delicious.

Unkie had left him a wad of cash so he could party with dudes his own age, and even maybe with chicks if he felt like it. Everything seemed to be going his way.

He planned to continue fucking Marlene until he had his million dollars in his pocket. She provided enough goodies in the way of clothing, champagne, reluctant but reliable cash gifts, the gym, the trainer...Yep. He'd keep Marlene company until independence day.

He planned to screw Lacy for as long as Henri was away. Lacy was a looker, and younger than either of his regular lovers. And as mistress to a series of rich dudes, she had to have tricks up her sleeves that maybe even Marlene didn't know about.

And if he had to spend some dough to romance that dude at the gym into his bed, well, "Thank you Unkie Al."

He began launching this golden period the morning after waving goodbye to his Unkie and his lover at LAX. He telephoned Lacy.

"Hi, Lacy. Were you up? Good. You know Henri asked me to keep you entertained while he's in New York. He left me a debit card so we can do the town. Would you like to go dancing tonight?"

Lacy told Rock she would love to go dancing. It had been a while since Henri had really taken her out. He tended to want to just make tepid love in the afternoon. He was big on fucking her feet and in sticking his tongue up her ass. Ho, hum. Most of all, he seemed to need to save himself for Rock later in the evening.

Rock had had to keep himself pretty much a homebody in the evenings for Henri as well.

Both Rock and Lacy felt they had been nightlife deprived. Both loved to dance. And Club Deep down on North Ivar was *the* place to go.

Date made. Rock would pick her up in Henri's Peugeot at eight. They would get a bite at Joseph's on Ivar and then on to Deep.

It sounded wonderful to Lacy. She hadn't been to Joseph's in ages. And she had never been to Deep. But most of all she hadn't had fresh meat since Henri started keeping her. Rock was one fine hunk of a youth. It made her mouth water to think of sucking an eighteen-year-old cock again. And having that vibrant tool spurting in her snatch...? It would be better than Christmas.

At ten o'clock Marlene came by for her morning visit.

"Well, Rock," she asked. "Are you getting it on with Henri's whore?"

"You mean the pretend wedding?"

"What else?" Marlene asked provocatively.

Rock wondered whether Marlene had figured out that he was planning to nail Lacy during Henri's absence. Not a subject he wanted to discuss. As a matter of fact, he still wanted to keep Marlene on the line. He finally had some money in his pocket but why not milk Marlene for as much as he could get?

"Forget about Lacy," he said. "With you in the room, I can't even think about other women. You are the most beautiful and glamorous woman I've ever known or ever hope to know."

Rock was good with the bullshit. And Marlene was always a sucker for it.

"I worked up a thirst getting here," she suggested, happy to change the subject toward getting some champagne poured.

Rock went through the phony routine of convincing her to have a sip of Veuve Clicquot. While she sipped, splayed out on his bed yet propped up on the large bolsters at the head, he turned on the CD player. He had pre-chosen "Let Me Entertain You" for Marlene's delectation. To that music, he disrobed in a fair imitation of male dancers like the Chippendales who do stripteases to audiences of horny women.

Marlene refilled her own champagne flute and lit her own cigarette so as not to interfere with the spectacle. Item by item, off came his articles of clothing. As each muscle group appeared from under its covering, he flexed and rippled the meat. It was a sight to make her twat clench.

When he was clad only in his jockey shorts, his dong was clearly outlined beneath the stretched cotton. Marlene had seen, felt, sucked and received that organ many, many times. But the sight of it hidden yet not hidden caused erotic shivers to run up and down her body. But the experience did not stop her from drinking her wine or inhaling her tobacco. Yet his act did hold her rapt attention.

At the right point in the music, "And we'll have a real good time," he came within reaching distance of her hands. She set aside her cigarette holder and her flute, and with a hand on each of his hips she slowly lowered his shorts. When the shorts fell to the floor and he stepped out of them, she took his balls in one hand and his semi-erect penis in the other and gently, oh so gently, led him up onto the bed. She directed his rising shaft to her mouth, reached to the side table, sipped some champagne, and with the bubbles still in her mouth slipped his manhood past her lips and into the bubbly wine.

It was his first cum of the day, so the orgasm was close to immediate. As the bubbly cum cascaded down her throat she thought she would swoon with joy.

Marlene slipped down from the bolstered pillows flat on the bed. Rock slid down to the foot of the bed. From there he began caressing her feet, beginning by licking the soles. He ran his tongue slowly up her legs.

When he started to nibble the sensitive skin of her inner thigh, her cunt juices dampened her panties. With his teeth, he removed her panties, telling her how fragrant her natural juices were.

With his tongue poised between her legs, he began to lick her flowing juices.

He was fully hard again, and began to pleasure himself with his fist as he drank in Marlene's nectar.

Marlene loved mouth music from her men. But her pussy yearned to be filled.

She told Rock to disengage himself from the "Y" and lie prone on the bed. He was ready for that kind of action and complied.

In slow motion Marlene impaled herself on his cock. His cock no sooner was fully imbedded in her than it twitched and spewed hot jism into her.

Marlene had other errands to attend to that morning. She had satisfied herself with Rock's talents, and after careful ablutions in the bathroom she left.

Strange to tell, her world-famous boobs had remained clothed throughout the entire interlude.

Rock had had enough frolic with mature womanhood. He relished a bit of sport that was nearer to his real preferences. So he was off to Vine Street and the gym.

In the locker room, Rock changed into his gym clothes.

When he got to the muscle room with its Powerflex and Nautilus machines and its free weights, he saw that Rip was involved training another dude. No problem. Rock had his regular schedule with Rip at 1:30 three times a week, and hadn't made an appointment for an extra session. So he worked out on the free weights without his personal trainer.

The stud he'd been eyeing was heading for the benches and Rock moseyed over to spot him. They exchanged glances and a tentative agreement was reached.

They spotted each other for an hour on bench presses. After an hour, each man was totally drenched in sweat. Rock followed his bench companion to the steam room. Each of them made sure the other got a quick eyeful.

When Rock went to the showers, he knew he was being followed. As they showered, they took discreet glances at each other's equipment. It was not acceptable to stare at other dudes in the showers. That is a definite branch of etiquette at Brewster's Gym. Each of them managed to take in enough to establish a bond of sorts.

Back in the locker room, Rock walked past the dude who was toweling off. All Rock said was "The Abbey." Either the stud would meet him later at the gay coffee bar on Robertson or he wouldn't. Rock had made the invitation. He'd see what happened. One never knows, does one?

At the Abbey, Rock settled down with a cup of coffee and sized up the dudes as they came in and went out. Checking out the meat would make the stop pleasant whether "Muscles" took up the invitation or not. There's more than one way to get lucky late in the morning.

Rock recognized his prospective date's bulge before he looked up to meet his eyes. A real hunk. See what happens.

The dude got a coffee and brought it toward Rock's table.

"That seat taken?"

"Been saving it for you."

The fellow put his cup on the table, sat down and extended his hand.

"Hank," he said, clasping Rock's hand with a wrenching grip.

"Rock."

"I know."

They sat in silence for a while, both watching the comings and goings of the other customers. Both were comfortable with the silence.

"Top or bottom?" Hank asked.

"Bottom," was Rock's response.

"Top," Hank said. An agreement was reached.

Rock was pretty sure which position Hank played from the beginning. He was so butch, a little older than Rock, and had angry eyes and a cruel mouth. Just the ticket.

After their curt exchange, the two men continued to sit silently, watching the meat parade.

Rock took his notepad and pen out of his pocket.

He wrote down "Emperor's Arms, 323," and laid the sheet of paper on the table.

"I know," was Hank's laconic answer. It seemed like a standard response.

It was clear than Hank knew a lot more about Rock than Rock knew about him.

They finished their coffees without exchanging a further word.

Hank got up and didn't so much as glance at Rock. He lumbered out of the coffee shop without a word. Rock liked the way his ass moved as he walked. Totally butch.

Rock got home and waited. It was his role to wait upon the pleasure of his coffee shop companion. Hank might come soon, or later, or not for days, or never. The prerogative was totally his. Rock left the door unlocked. He knew the rules.

After a half-hour wait, the door opened. No knock. No ring. Hank's figure loomed in the doorway, his body clad in black leather, cap, boots, and all. Rock figured he'd landed a good one.

"What kind of beer you got in this dump?"

"Bud."

"Get outta here. Run, do not walk, to a liquor store. Get a six-pack of Coors for me. When you get back, you can suck on your goddam Bud if you want. And I want you to get back here drenched in sweat. Understand? Run both ways!"

Rock hustled out, ran as instructed four blocks to the liquor store, bought the brew Hank liked, and ran back to the apartment. He hoped he was drenched enough to please his new lover.

Apparently he was sweaty enough on his return to please his leather-clad companion. Without being asked, he opened a bottle of the Coors and offered it to Hank.

"Take off your goddam clothes," Hank ordered.

Rock did as he was told.

"Now unzip my fly," Hank commanded.

Rock complied and dropped to his knees without being told to do so.

Without another word, he took his lover's angry, demanding cock into his mouth and sucked as Hank downed his beer.

"Deeper, Asshole!"

Rock dared not gag.He was into this, but did not want any bruises he would have to explain away later to Lacy.

By the time Hank lumbered out of the apartment Rock was exhausted. But he had survived unbloodied and unbruised.

CHAPTER SIX

Rock had made the necessary reservations for the evening.

He picked Lacy up in the Peugeot at seven-thirty. She was obviously ready for a party, as shown in part by the overnight bag she carried with her. Rock understood the message.

They arrived at Joseph's on North Ivar at eight. Valet parking, of course.

The bulk of the diners seemed to be young star-struck couples attracted to the restaurant in part because Britney and Kevin had met there. Rock chose it because that kind of clientele flocked there. And because there was dancing as well as dining.

At the table, Rock and Lacy decided on Rob Roy cocktails.

"Could we have that prepared with Jonnie Walker Blue label?"

They could.

Joseph's famous hummus and pita bread seemed like the perfect appetizer to bolster the Scotch.

Lacy decided on a Caesar salad and the grilled lamb chops with garlic mashed potatoes served with a mint au jus and baked tomato. Rock opted for the avocado and grapefruit salad, filet mignon on the bone with dauphinois potatoes and garlic spinach.

A discussion with the sommelier revealed that there was one bottle left in the cellar of the one-and-a-half liter bottle of Marilyn Velvet Collection, 2002, a mélange of Cabernet Sauvignon, Merlot, and Syrah grapes. At three hundred-fifty dollars, Rock and Lacy thought it a steal. Particularly considering the fancy label with the picture of the movie star on it. And especially when paid for on Henri's debit card.

For dessert they decided on the baklava. The sommelier assured them that a bottle of Muscat de Beaumes de Venise Rouge Fenouillet, 1996, would be the perfect accompaniment. Oh, how right he was!

The DJ arrived while they dined and they found the Hip-Hop, Reggae, and R&B very danceable.

The evening had begun joyously, thanks to the very healthy balance on Henri's debit card.

The dancing at Joseph's warmed the couple up for the next stop at Deep.

The drive from Joseph's to Club Deep was a matter of minutes. Rock had arranged for reserved seating with bottle service. Which meant that when he and Lacy arrived at their table at ten o'clock, there was an ice bucket holding a bottle of La Grande Dame Brut '96. Rock had been assured that once they had killed the bottle, another one, also pre-chilled, would take its place. They drank. They found their way from their VIP room through the maze of mirrors that led to the dance floor. The dance music was retro with Eighties and Disco. It phased to Soul and then to Hip-Hop.

They danced. They drank. They swallowed ecstasy. They kissed. They rubbed bodies. They imbibed the fun-loving swing of Hollywood in its decadent glory.

By one o'clock they had somehow finished off three bottles of the exquisite bubbly, danced their hearts out, and, though fully clothed, had made intimate contact with nearly every erogenous zone of each other's body.

Fortunately, the drive from North Ivar to the Emperor's Arms was short enough not to overly tax Rock's altered reflexes from the alcoholic excesses of the evening.

Their lovemaking back at his apartment was a tribute to his youth and stamina and to her experience and fortitude.

The next three days were passed in a delirious haze of champagne, dancing, cocktails, partying, coke, fucking, reds, bar hopping, pot, sucking, ecstasy, mixed doubles, speed, gambling, meth, clubs, blues, dining, crack, brawls...

When they were at Rock's place, the door was always left unlocked. The drop-in guests included Marlene, Hank, people they had picked up at parties, people whose faces they did not remember, some of whom had memorable bodies, and wackos. It was a memorable omni-sexual romp. The money left for their entertainment by Henri and Unkie Al was beginning to get stretched to the limit in those three days.

The fourth morning of the constant partying was intruded upon by a figure at the door. Lacy was busily engaged in sucking Rock's cock when the door opened. It was immediately clear to the couple that the visitor was not Marlene. It was clearly male. It was not Hank. Shorter and stouter. It was...

"Hello, Unkie Al. What are you doing here?"

Rock lost his hardon instantly. Lacy pulled a sheet over their nakedness.

Unkie was less astounded than amused. He calmly sat down in a chair and talked to them in his easy, drawling fashion.

"It looks like the honeymoon began before the wedding. Exactly the way I did it, both times I got married. Don't be embarrassed. Unkie Al didn't just fall off the turnip truck."

He went on to explain that when he got to Shanghai the Chinese were ready to negotiate. When they really wanted something, they were easy to deal with. They wanted copper and Madrazo could and would supply it for a price agreeable to both. There was no need for him to stay on to work out the details of payment, delivery, and legalities. Unkie left his chief financial officer, his logistics genius, and his legal counsel in China to hammer out the fine points. He had negotiated the basic contract. A contract favorable to both parties.

He told Rock and Lacy he could have stayed on in China and enjoyed the lavish hospitality of the country. But he knew the young couple would want him back to attend the wedding. So he hopped the next plane to LAX and here he was. Weren't they tickled pink?

Pink!

"So. When's the wedding to be?"

Neither of the fiancés was thinking too clearly that morning. And Unkie's sudden arrival did nothing to clear up the miasma that constant hedonism had stirred up in their brains.

Lacy's mental processes stumbled about for an answer.

"Friday," she blurted out. It was the first word that emerged from the confused state of her mind. She wasn't really sure what day of the week had actually dawned at present. But at least Unkie's question had been answered.

"Capital!" Unkie exclaimed. "Where are you two going to do the deed?"

Rock's brain struggled for an answer to the difficult question.

"Las Vegas?" he either said or asked.

Unkie took it for a statement rather than a question.

"Dandy! I love Vegas. Now listen. Why don't I treat you two to breakfast at the Griddle Café down at Sunset and Fairfax? Best French press coffee I've found in town. The pancakes and eggs are as good as I've eaten in Hollywood. I'll wait for you in the lobby. You finish off what you were doing, get yourselves dressed, and I'll see you downstairs."

Unkie Al breezed out of there without waiting for an answer.

The couple was incapable of "finishing what they were doing."

In a daze they got out of bed, took care of their ablutions, got dressed, and morosely headed out to meet Unkie for breakfast. Neither was quite sure about how to resolve a very perplexing new reality.

Unkie Al made himself comfortable in the richly appointed lobby of the building. He chuckled to himself as he thought of the young man he knew to be his son-bar-sinister getting an early-morning blow job from his prospective bride. He began to daydream about some of the more memorable blowjobs he had enjoyed over his extensive lovelife.

In the midst of a smile occasioned by the memory of a nubile beauty in Memphis many years back, he was roused out of his thoughts by a familiar voice in a famous French accent.

"Mister Pughworthy. Imagine meeting you here! I thought you were in China."

Unkie Al stood up to shake hands.

"'Pon my soul! Mister Gabin. I am equally surprised. I was sure you were in New York."

The two men shook hands, then sat down to chat.

Unkie Al explained the ease of negotiations with the Chinese. He mentioned his haste to get back to Hollywood to be present at the nuptials.

Henri was amused at the turn of events, but at the same time was somewhat distressed at the predicament now facing his friend and lover.

Henri explained that when he got to New York the backers of The Mad Lover of Notre-Dame were in a gigantic argument with the producers. Before they were able to begin even the first readings, much less rehearsals, the bottom fell out of the financing and the whole deal was called off.

Henri had returned to Hollywood unannounced to surprise his friends that he was back in circulation. His luggage was to be delivered by the airline later that day.

"I'm sorry you didn't get a chance to do the show on Broadway, though," Unkie said.

"Yes. It was a good opportunity for me to break out of the rut I'm in. A movie actor really needs to tread the boards, make touch with a live audience, and all that. But there'll be other opportunities."

There was a pause in the conversation because Unkie Al had nothing to add.

Henri asked, "Why are you sitting down here in the lobby?"

"I'm waiting for Rock to get dressed. We're going out for a late breakfast at the Griddle Café. Won't you join us?"

"Thank you," Henri answered. "I'd be delighted. I love their coffee. And I doubt there's a better breakfast served in the whole state."

"Great," Unkie said. "Rock can tell us all about the wedding plans. Did you know he and Lacy are getting married on Friday? They'll be so happy you're back here in time to be at the celebration."

"Hmmm. Friday you say? Do you know where the ceremony's taking place?"

"In Vegas," Unkie enthused. "A fun city, that."

"Yes," Henri said, wondering what kind of jam his lover had gotten himself into. "Real fun."

Unkie was caught up in the situation.

"From what I've seen, Friday isn't a moment too soon, either."

"Why do you say that?"

"Oh, nothing" Unkie backtracked. "I spoke without thinking. Forget I said anything."

"No, no," Henri urged, smelling a rat. "It's all right. Do you know something?"

Unkie relented.

"Well, maybe it's O.K. You're Rock's best friend and Lacy's relative. And you're a man of the world. I'll bet you'll be best man at the wedding or give the bride away now that you're back on the Coast. He'll probably tell you what he and Lacy were up to anyway. The sort of things guys confide in each other."

Henri was really intrigued. Something was definitely up.

"Sure," Henri coaxed. "Rock and I don't have any secrets from each other. What are best friends for, after all?"

"Promise you won't tell anyone?"

"Absolutely! I promise!"

"Particularly you won't tell Rock. It could cause problems between him and me if he thought I was a blabbermouth."

Henri promised his lips were sealed.

"Well," Unkie Al proceeded. "It's too good to keep all to myself. You know Rock is a virile, robust young guy."

"So he tells me," Henri confided.

"It's true? He just couldn't wait until the wedding."

"He couldn't wait...? Henri said, beginning to get the picture.

"I went bursting into his room this morning. The door was unlocked so I just went in without thinking. And guess what I saw?"

"I can't imagine," said Henri, imagining all too well.

"He was getting his wick trimmed."

"By...?"

"By Lacy of course. Rock's true blue. You know how he is. He wouldn't cheat."

"You actually saw Lacy sucking Rock's cock?"

"Isn't that a hoot? I told hem it didn't embarrass me. I was blown lots of times by both of my brides to be. No need to be hypocritical about it, is there?"

"You are certainly right about that," Henri said.

There was one word in his mind. Revenge! He had trusted Rock with Lacy. Even left him a couple of thousand dollars to keep her from the Hollywood wolves. And Rock had betrayed him. Rock would pay. And so would Lacy. He needed time to coldly think out a sweet revenge for them both.

"Look, Mister Pughworthy. From what you say, the two lovebirds must be up in Rock's apartment right now."

"Yep. They should be down here any moment."

"I don't want to embarrass them by being here when they come down together. They might feel they have to explain things away. And I want Rock to tell me about this in his own sweet time. So, tell you what. I'll sneak out of here and walk into the Griddle Café in twenty minutes or so, as if I was just dropping in for a bite. I'll explain about the Broadway show being cancelled, and they can tell me about the wedding."

"Capital idea," Unkie Al agreed. "We men of the world need to be discreet, don't we?"

"Don't we just?" Henri agreed, shook hands with Unkie, and left the building.

Henri's mind set to work immediately. What would be the perfect revenge for the two betrayers? Particularly for Rock. After all, Lacy was a whore. What could you expect? But it was Rock he had trusted.

What was it that Rock wanted most? To make it in the movies? Probably. What was it that Rock was concerned about? What did he want to avoid? Marrying Lacy. He needed to avoid marrying a known whore. He wanted the money from the trust but needed to avoid actually marrying Lacy. He'd be the laughing stock of Hollywood and his career would be finished before it ever got started.

The trick was to make sure Rock married Lacy without either of them knowing it was happening. Or, Plan B would be to somehow make sure that Rock didn't get married and have the trust money go up in smoke.

Hmmm. Las Vegas wedding. A plan formed in Henri's head. Rock and Lacy were just stupid enough to fall for it.

By the time Henri got to the café, Rock, Lacy and Unkie were already seated at a table. And Henri's plan was fully fledged.

Rock caught sight of Henri as he walked in the door.

"Lacy, Unkie, look! That's Henri coming in here."

Unkie expressed surprise, as agreed upon with Henri.

"I'll be damned," he said. I thought Mister Gabin was in New York."

Henri feigned surprise when he saw the three sitting there and walked up to the table.

"Fancy meeting you three here this morning!"

Henri took a seat at the table and everyone gushed with surprise, wonderment, and happiness that they were all together. Rock and Lacy had to keep gushing through the remnants of the fog they were still carrying in their heads. Unkie explained to Henri again about the China deal and its early happy conclusion. Henri told about the Broadway brouhaha.

The others had already ordered. Henri ordered French toast, bacon, and coffee.

Unkie took it upon himself to break the delightful news.

"It's too bad about the show not getting produced in New York, Mister Gabin. But there is a compensation."

Henri expressed interest.

"Did you know this couple is getting married Friday?"

"No," Henri enthused. "I hadn't heard. Congratulations you two. So I got back here in time to attend. Where are you two going to tie the knot?"

Rock gulped and mentioned "Las Vegas."

"Vegas!" Henri said."What a great choice. Am I invited?"

Unkie answered for the couple.

"Are you invited? Of course. I'll bet you'll be part of the wedding party. Am I right, Rock?"

"Yeah," Rock answered without much enthusiasm.

As they ate their breakfast, Rock and Lacy gradually loosened up and showed some genuine animation.

Rock told Henri, "I've really missed you, Pal."

Henri answered, "Sure. Me too. I see you've taken good care of Lacy in my absence."

"Yeah, sure. We agreed to meet here for breakfast with Unkie Al."

As he finished his breakfast, Unkie said, "Well, this looks like a happy reunion of friends. I've got to get going. There'll be some faxes coming in for me from my associates in China. How about the three of you meeting me for dinner tonight?"

The three agreed. Unkie said he had enough pull to get reservations for them at L'Orangerie for eight-thirty. They said they'd be there.

When Unkie was gone, Rock unloaded on Henri.

"Whew! Man! Henri, I'm in real deep shit. You saw what happened. Unkie's back and expects a marriage on Friday."

Lacy chimed in.

"And there's no way a wedding's going to happen. Out of the question."

Henri was ready for this.

"There's always a solution," he said. "Good thing I got back when I did. How did you happen to say you're getting married Friday? And in Vegas?"

Lacy said, "I had to tell him something. That was the first idea that popped into my mind."

Henri appeared to ponder.

"Vegas, huh? I've got an idea. I can't leave you two people I care about most in the whole world to stew. Listen to this and see what you think."

Rock was relieved.

"Good old Henri. Our real friend."

"You bet," Henri agreed. "As faithful to the two of you as you are to me. Now look. Unkie Al is looking for a wedding. So we have to give him a wedding."

Lucy and Rock showed wonder.

Rock showed his colors first.

"Lacy's fine. But she's a whore. She's the last person in the world I'd marry."

Henri remonstrated.

"Not marry Lacy? She's such a faithful mistress. She'd be a faithful wife."

Lacy took umbrage at Rock's statement.

"Me a whore? You're nothing but a spoiled rotten little twerp male starlet. And going after Unkie's money. You're a bigger whore than I am."

Henri took the avuncular role.

"Now, now, children. Don't fight. I wouldn't have my most trusted friend marry my ever faithful Lacy for the world. That's not what I'm talking about. I'm talking about a fake marriage. A bit of acting to fool Unkie Al."

Rock latched onto the idea.

"Sounds good, Pal. What's the plan?"

"We go to Vegas on Thursday. There's the Graceland Wedding Chapel right on the Strip."

"Yeah, I've seen it," Rock said. "It's famous."

"Well," Henri continued. "The gimmick there is that the marrying preachers are all dressed like Elvis."

"I've heard about that," Lacy said.

"Well," Henri told them. "I've got a good friend in Vegas. Guy I've known for years. He's an Elvis impersonator at Harrah's."

"One of those Elvis-preacher guys?" Rock asked.

"Not at all. Ken's an entertainer, pure and simple. Sings well. Plays a fine guitar. What I can do is get the Elvis-preacher to step aside and get Ken to do the ceremony. Unkie goes with the two of you to the Clark County Courthouse where you get the marriage license. I go to Graceland Chapel and arrange for the preacher to step aside with a bribe. Ken steps in, says the words. No way is he licensed to marry people. Nothing legal at all about the ceremony. Later you burn the license or keep it as a souvenir and you're home free."

Rock and Lacy bought it.

With that out of the way, Henri asked the couple what they had been doing while he was away. Rock gave him a greatly expurgated version of their activities and returned Henri's debit card to him. There was a glimmer in his brain that when Henri received the statement for the card it might tell him more than Rock wanted told. How they had possibly spent that much money in so few days. The glimmer faded into the cloud that still hung over his brain cells.

Henri went back to the Emperor's Arms with Rock, telling Lacy he'd see her later in the day.

When Henri got Rock alone in his apartment, he gave him the roughest fucking he'd ever given anyone in his life.

Later, Lacy was the recipient of the most potent lovemaking she'd ever received from Henri.

In his anger, Henri found that he was as virile as a teenager. He'd never before fucked in anger. He liked it. It gave him the true passion of a great French lover.

CHAPTER SEVEN

The wedding party consisted of eight people. The prospective bride and groom, Rock and Lacy, would be staying in a suite at the Venetian reserved and paid for by Unkie as a wedding gift. He reserved a suite there for himself and a certain dancer, Elaine, from the Tropicana Folies Bergeres. Henri took a room overlooking the dancing waters at the Bellagio. He was designated as best man and had a wedding ring with him.

Henri had issued an invitation to Marlene, letting her in on his wicked trick. He knew she would be amused. Marlene reserved a suite at the Luxor, and brought along a young man named Lance whom she had chosen as Rock's replacement. She had checked Lance out and found he was not only quite trainable but had a tongue to die for.

Rock wanted his butch lover Hank at the festivities and took a room for him at the Paris. He planned to make love with Henri for the last time following the ceremony. But he wanted to spend his wedding night with Hank.

Lacy rode to Las Vegas in the Peugeot with Henri. She was, of course, still his mistress.

Rock rode with Unkie on the plane.

The others got there by car, train, or plane.

Thursday night, all members of the wedding party were checked into their accommodations. Lacy had to spend the night with Henri, of course, which left Rock free to party with Hank. It was a night of revelry for everyone.

Lacy was amazed at Henri's new-found libido. He was stiff as an iron pipe and was punishing in his lovemaking. She wondered what New York had done for the man's cock. Not bad. But second rate to the eighteen-year-old tool that Rock wielded.

On Friday morning, Unkie Al accompanied Rock and Lacy to the Clark County Courthouse in downtown Las Vegas. Weddings are a mass business in Vegas, and there was a half-hour wait in line to get to the issuing clerk. Unkie beamed when the license was issued.

At the same time, Henri was at Graceland Chapel. He had called ahead a few days before to reserve a time for the fifteen minute ceremony. He had pre-paid by credit card, of course, but was there to assure himself that everything was in order for the ceremony that would wed his lover to his whore.

By ten o'clock, when Lacy, Rock, and Unkie arrived at the chapel by taxi, the guests were sitting in the pews. Marlene, Lance, and Hank were enjoying a ribald conversation. Unkie's date, Elaine, chose not to attend and was sleeping in at the Venetian.

A strum on a guitar alerted all that the ceremonies were about to begin. Reverend Amos Knorr, looking like a somewhat degenerate Elvis Presley, sideburns, jump suit, and all, began to sing and play *Love Me Tender.*

Rock whispered to Henri:

"That guy playing Elvis. He's your friend?"

"Trust me," Henri answered. "Just an entertainer from Harrah's. You have nothing to worry about.

"You're a real pal," Rock said, satisfied that all was well.

Lacy, Rock, and Henri walked solemnly up the aisle to the altar.

When Reverend Amos came to the end of his song, "*And I always will,*" he set his guitar down against the wall. He didn't pay much attention to Lacy or Henri. But he did check Rock out, up and down. He appeared to like what he saw.

With great solemnity, Henri joined Lacy's and Rock's hands together. He then stepped back, left the couple at the altar, and sat in the pew directly behind Marlene and Lance. He envied Marlene her new boyfriend. A real hunk.

Reverend Amos launched into his routine.

"Dearly beloved. We are met here in Graceland Chapel to join this man and this woman in the bonds of holy matrimony.

"Do you, Rock, take this here woman to be your lawfully wedded wife?"

"Sure do, Elvis," Rock answered. He was enjoying what he believed to be a farce.

Henri and Marlene clapped and the others in the pews joined them. Rock turned towards the congregation and took a bow.

When he turned back, the reverend whispered to Rock.

"You are one cute groom. Do you happen to swing?"

Rock looked at the bulge in the reverend's pants. Clearly a falsie. The reverend wasn't his type and he knew he'd literally have his hands full with Henri and then with Hank for the rest of the day anyway.

He whispered back, "Sorry, Bub. My dance card is filled for today."

Reverend Amos shrugged his shoulders. He was used to being turned down. You don't get much action as a marrying Elvis in Las Vegas.

Time to wrap it up.

When the reverend asked who had the ring, Henri realized he should have stayed up at the altar. His familiar French accented voice ran out over the chapel.

"I have the ring, Reverend Sir," and stepped up to the altar with all the pomp the sacred ceremony deserved.

Rock took the ring from Henri and winked at him conspiratorially. He slipped the ring on Lacy's finger. The reverend pronounced them man and wife, took up his guitar, strummed an introduction, and sang.

Wise men say 'Only fools rush in,'
But I can't help falling in love with you.
Shall I stay? Would it be a sin
If I can't help falling in love with you.

Reverend Amos had caught sight of Hank in the congregation and was clearly singing the song not to the bride and groom but to that "bad boy" in leather.

Hank knew there would be lots of time on his hands before Rock could get to the Paris. He thought it might be great sport to brutally humiliate that Elvis asshole. And maybe even beat the shit out of him if it looked like that was what the slave-type wanted.

When the preacher and the dude finished their conversation, Henri approached Reverend Amos. The reverend signed the marriage license and gave it to Henri. With glee, Henri took the legal document to Unkie.

"Here, Mister Pughworthy," he said. "No doubt the trust that holds money will want to record this."

Unkie looked at the certificate and smiled.

"That's terrific, Mister Gabin. This document proves Rock is straight."

"Nothing gay about our boy Rock," Henri laughed.

The tiny congregation was being encouraged to leave the chapel. The next couple was getting ready for its turn. The next Reverend Elvis in rotation was tuning his guitar.

Henri had made arrangements at the Baccarat Bar at the Bellagio for the reception. The Baccarat was Vegas' prime venue for mini-receptions. They provide Perrier-Jouet Champagne at a very favorable price for wedding parties. And it is a very convivial spot.

Everyone came to the reception: The bride and groom, the best man, and the rich uncle of course. Unkie contacted his date, Elaine, and she hustled over for the party. Reverend Amos made sure he was in a booth with Hank. Marlene and Lance were cuddled in a separate booth of their own. Marlene was a good sport and drank the free-flowing Perrier-Jouet rather than her accustomed Veuve Clicquot.

When Elaine arrived at the Baccarat Bar, Unkie excused himself from the booth he was in to join her at a separate booth. That left Henri, Lacy and Rock together so Henri could drop his bomb.

"Nice guy, your Unkie Al," he said.

"Yeah," Rock agreed. "A prince."

"Did you know I met him in the lobby at the Emperor's Arms when I got back from New York?" Henri asked.

The champagne must have been fogging up Rock's mind because he couldn't quite process that. Henri saw his confusion.

"Yes, Rock," he said. "He was sitting in the lobby waiting for you two to come down and join him. So he could take you to the Griddle Café for breakfast. You remember the Griddle Café , don't you?"

Both Rock and Lacy nodded their heads, but didn't seem able to coordinate time and place from what Henri was saying.

Henri put a hand on Rock's shoulder.

"I knew I could trust you, Rock. I knew that if I left Lacy in your care I wouldn't have to worry about any unfaithfulness from either of you. Right?"

An uneasiness settled around the booth. Rock and Lacy gulped down several swallows of the Perrier-Jouet. Henri's tone was growing more ironic. Something was up.

"Imagine my surprise that morning," Henri went on, "when I found your Unkie waiting for the two of you to come down from your room. I didn't want to embarrass my two most faithful friends and lovers in the whole world by being in the lobby when you descended. You might have felt it necessary to explain how you happened to be together at that hour of the morning."

"Oh, I can explain," Rock said immediately. "You see, Lacy had come up to my place to knock on the door to wake me up..."

"Tut-tut," Henri scoffed. "No need to explain, my boy. I would trust your explanation, whatever it was. That is, as far as I would trust you two. But, then, on the other hand, I might have reason to suspect your explanation."

"Why?" Rock and Lacy said, exuding innocence.

"Because Unkie spilled the beans."

"Beans?"

"About walking into your apartment, Rock."

"Walking in..."

"While my mistress was busily sucking your cock."

Rock and Lacy had nothing to say to that. Busted! Busted good!

"So," Henri said when he had allowed for a dramatic pause. "I decided not to get angry."

"That's great," Rock said.

"I decided to get revenge."

There was no response to that. Henri let his statement hang there in the champagne fumes for a while.

"Someone once got very upset with me. A similar situation to yours. And his revenge was to make it clear that a certain young lady and I deserved each other. I recalled that event when I found out about you two. And it is my revenge on you two. I have arranged for a talentless twerp to marry a whore. You two certainly deserve each other."

"You mean the wedding ceremony...?"

"Was real," Henri confirmed. "You can ask Reverend Amos over there."

The three of them looked over at the booth where the reverend and Hank had refused the champagne and were drinking Coors. Not only were they downing brews, but they were involved in a very deep and passionate kiss. It broke Rock's heart to see his hunk making out with that fake Elvis.

Rock didn't have to ask the preacher. He knew that what Henri said was true.

Very satisfied with himself, Henri got up from the booth and without so much as a "farewell" or a "go to Hell" turned his back on the couple and walked confidently to the booth where Marlene and Lance were enjoying champagne and stealthy intimacies. Marlene's stud-muffin, Lance, was certainly an eyeful.

Might the young man possibly swing both ways?

Rock and Lacy, the bride and groom, were left alone in their booth.

"Damn!" Rock said.

"Look at the bright side," Lacy suggested.

"What bright side?"

"The last few days have been a ball, haven't they, Rock?"

"The best time I've ever had," Rock admitted.

"Now that we're married, and have two million dollars to spend, the party can go on until we've lived up every penny. You've got eyes for our boy in black leather. No problem. I've got eyes the dancing girl. Also, no problem. We can be married and still be AC/DC all we want. If the marriage had been fake, Unkie would have found out eventually some way. And the fortune would never have been yours.

"Hubby, Dear. You and I are going to have ourselves the time of our lives."

"I'll drink to that!" Rock said and the two laughed heartily.

"Let the good times keep on rollin'."

The two million dollars did not last very long. Rock and Lacy were geniuses at spending money on a good time.

PART TWO

HOLLYWOOD MERRY-GO-ROUND

CHAPTER ONE
WILLA ON CAMERA:

Hi! I'm Willa Roberts. Well, that is, I *was* Willa Roberts. I used to be married to Rob Roberts. You know – the famous movie producer and screen writer. He calls himself an *auteur.*

This apartment complex you see me in? I own it. That's right. Rob bought it for me as a wedding present. Some present, isn't it? This is one of the most famous apartment houses in Hollywood, the Emperor's Arms. There's even an old Hollywood joke about it. Newcomer to town asks a Hollywood type, "Where's the Emperor's Arms?" Answer: "Around the Empress' neck."

In the old days, that used to wow 'em. It takes more than that to make 'em laugh now days.

This apartment complex was built in 1924. D.W. Griffeth, the old silent movie honcho, was one of the original investors in the property. He lived up in the penthouse back in the twenties.

Mae West, the sexy blonde actress? She lived up in that penthouse later, and threw parties like you wouldn't believe. Later she bought the Ravenswood Arms down in Larchmont and lived in the penthouse there.

Errol Flynn, the actor with a talent for sex on and off the stage? He rented Apartment 222 in this very building in the thirties. That apartment has a special name to this day. "Jailbait Heaven." I don't know what that means, but a lot of Hollywood visitors come here just to look at the door to 222.

If I told you who's living in the penthouse today, you'd be surprised. But I'm the landlady. And I'm not telling. That's part of the promise I made with the movie star up there when he rented the place.

Rob, my ex, took care of all the management side of the rental business here back when we were married. He did the work. I got the money for my own little account. So I could shop, shop, shop. No questions asked. Talk about a happy deal!

This room where they're filming me is Apartment 123. And the merry-go-round started here in this very room.

The story begins with Maurice and me making love. Not in this actual room. In the bedroom through that door over there. When I say "Maurice," I mean Maurice Delatour, the famous French actor. Actually his real name is Barney Glasscock and he came to Hollywood from Cucamonga, California. But he does a French accent so believable everyone thinks he comes from Paris, France. That's a laugh, isn't it?

When Maurice and I got together, he could be either Maurice or Barney. He usually let me choose who he was going to be.

Anyway. This one day I was telling you about, Maurice and I were in the bedroom behind that door there. I wanted him to do his Maurice Delatour shtick. I considered that kind of romantic back then. He was telling me he was trying to get some producer to re-do the Pepe le Moko movie. With him as Pepe, of course.

"Who is Pepe le Moko?" I asked.

"Who is Pepe le Moko?!" Maurice exclaimed. "It's just the choicest role in all French cinema for a leading man. That's all. He was played by Jean Gabin in French in 1937."

"Never heard of him. That was somewhat before my time," I said. "Besides, foreign films leave me cold."

"Then," Maurice went on, not to be stopped by my interruption. "The very next year, in 1938, Charles Boyer played the part of Pepe here in Hollywood, in English. And Hedy Lamarr played his girlfriend Gaby."

"Even in English, it's all ancient history to me," I scoffed. "I'm just not that much into old movies in any language."

Maurice was unfazed by my indifference to Pepe le Moko and surged right on ahead.

"How about this line?" he asked. "It's from the movie, the one in

English. It's an absolutely immortal line. Pepe le Moko says to this Gaby with whom he wants to make mad passionate love, 'Come wiz me to ze Casbah.'"

"*That's* the big line?" I jibed. It didn't even make sense to me.

"Yes. 'Come wiz me to ze Casbah,' is how it was in the Charles Boyer film. But that was not as grand as in the original with Jean Gabin."

"What the Hell is a Casbah?" I asked. As if I cared.

He goes, "The Casbah is the native Arab quarter in Algiers."

I go, "What's Algiers?"

Maurice can be very condescending. He nearly patted me on the head when he explained, "Algiers is a city in North Africa."

"Oh," I said. Like I cared?

It's nice to get a geography lesson from your lover. I guess.

"Anyway," Maurice forged on. "The old Arab quarter of Algiers is called the Casbah. But the heart of the Casbah is the Suq."

"The what?" I say, kinda taken aback. But also all of a sudden kinda interested.

"Suq," he says.

"Okay," I go, playful like. "I will. But you gotta wait. I want to hear the rest of the story."

"What Pepe le Moko said to Gaby in the 1937 French version was 'Come wiz me to ze Suq."

"How could a girl refuse an invitation like that?" I asked.

"She couldn't. So she did."

"Suq?" I asked.

"Suq!" Maurice insisted.

"Okay, Maurice. You be Pepe and I'll be Gaby. Shoot me the line."

"Come wiz me to ze Suq."

"I sure will," I joked. "But first you'll have to drop your drawers."

Maurice was real serious about that Pepe le Moko crap. But when I told him to drop his drawers he snapped out of it real fast

After a while he said, "This apartment is great. Is it for rent?"

I told him it was.

He went back to using his Barney voice. Which was the right one for just relaxing.

Maurice knew how I like to joke, so he kept his pants on. At least for the moment.

But later we both did disrobe and hopped into bed. As a lover, the "Great French Lover" wasn't really French. And he wasn't really great.

But he wasn't all that bad, either. And I did get a French kiss. And he got a great "Suq." If I do say so myself, I give great head.

Barney/Maurice had rented a little love nest over in Topanga Canyon in a kind of cheesy apartment building on Topanga Canyon Boulevard. We'd been meeting each other there for sex romps for a couple of months. It suited the purpose, but I could tell that Maurice was considering this apartment at the Emperor's Arms as a better place for our love nest. It certainly would be handier than cruising out to Topanga Canyon when we wanted to get it on.

I liked the idea of this place being handy for me. And I got a kick out of thinking we'd be fucking each other here in Number 123 while my hubby Rob was working away right above us in 223. I believe they call that irony.

Maurice knew I owned the building. And I'd told him before that Rob took care of all the business end.

He said, "I'll drop by your place upstairs later on in the day and tell Rob I want to rent this place. Then we can come back tonight for a soirée."

I told him I thought the idea of renting the place was cool. But that if he rented it that afternoon, we wouldn't be able to use it that evening.

"Why not?" he asked.

"When you rent it," I told him. "Rob will call Mrs. Gustavson, the cleaning lady, to get the place ready for you, the new tenant. She could come barging in here any time this evening. So, if you want us to get together tonight I'll have to meet you at the Topanga Canyon love nest."

Maurice understood and said that the sooner he rented this place the sooner we could use it for our trysts. He loved that word "tryst." But matinée and soirée had a nice exotic sound to them, too. When we were ready to leave, Maurice said he'd be seeing me later in the day when he came back to sign the papers to rent this apartment.

"And then I'll see you tonight at Topanga Canyon," I told him.

He switched back to being Maurice with the French accent. He liked to be Maurice when he thought he was being particularly suave.

"I'll be ready," he answered. "I just can't get enough of you."

One thing I liked about Maurice. He was a smooth talker.

CHAPTER TWO
ROB ON CAMERA:

Hello. I'm Rob Roberts, the world famous auteur. You've seen my movies, of course. Who hasn't? And now here I am in person.

This is the livingroom of my apartment here on Larchmont Boulevard. I used to live over at the Emperor's Arms in Hollywood. But after my wife and I split up I moved here.

You probably want to know how I write those fabulous movies of mine that you've all seen. People are always asking me about that.

"Do you write at a computer? Or on an old fashioned typewriter? Or how about pen and ink?"

Everyone wants to know. And I always tell them I dictate my scripts into a machine. And that usually satisfies them. But I usually don't go on to tell them more about my dictation machine. It's my natural modesty, I guess.

Well, here it is folks! For the first time on film, I'll demonstrate how I compose my terrific scripts.

I sit at this desk here. See that big microphone up on the wall? Whether I'm sitting here at the desk or pacing around the room it picks up every golden word I utter. As I conjure up dialog for a script I'm working on, I just spit out the words. They get caught in that microphone and are transmitted to the tape recorder in this cabinet here. Isn't that astounding?

Naturally I can't bother to keep turning the recorder on and off manually. That would interfere with my creative juices. So I invented this unbelievably clever idea. The machine is voice activated. Right! Voice activated!

You see, all I have to do is say the word "Love" and the machine turns on. It records my every word. And when I want to turn it off, like if I get interrupted by someone or something, all I have to do is say "Hate" and it turns off.

I've written the screen plays for my last three movies by simply spewing my ideas into this gadget and then editing the tape on my PC over there.

As it turns out, this recorder can also serve as a spy machine. It wasn't designed for that purpose, but it got used once as a spookmachine anyway. I'll tell you about that pretty soon.

Back when my ex-wife Willa and I were living at the Emperor's Arms, I used our livingroom as my workroom. This machine was set up there. You wouldn't particularly notice it when you came in since most of the recording devices are in that cabinet.

But, enough about my recording device. I want to tell you about my ex, Willa. She was a doll. At least I thought she was. She told me she was a virgin when I married her. And I believed her. On our wedding night I asked her how come, if she was a virgin, she didn't have a hymen. She told me she'd ruptured it in an ice skating accident.

Ice skating accident, hah! But I believed her. One of the troubles with us geniuses. We'll fall for anything. I thought she was the sweetest, most naïve little gal I'd ever met.

And I believed she was the most faithful wife anyone ever had. And me? I was pretty faithful to her. Considering. When I'm casting for one of my pictures, I've got to fuck around a bit with the starlets. It's expected. What else is a casting couch good for? But other than the casting couch I was as faithful as Methuselah.

On this day I'm telling you about I was dictating the script for *Showdown in Loredo*. You've probably seen it. The critics hated it. They hate all my stuff. The public – you – loved it, of course. It was Part Two of my famous tetralogy. What a concept!

I was working out that scene where Crusher, who plays Big Dick McGoon, comes staggering out of the Last Chance Saloon just as Tex steps out of the sheriff's office. A great scene, if I do say so myself.

I was wondering which man the camera should focus on when Willa, my ex, comes barging into the room. I hastened to say "Hate" to turn off the machine. She didn't notice. She's used to me shouting out all kinds of things when I'm composing.

"What are you working on now?" she asked.

"It's Part Two of my tetralogy," I said.

"You mean it's a sequel to that last stupid Crusher and Tex movie you made?"

"Stupid?" I responded. "That *stupid* fucking movie grossed three million the first week."

Willa often bad-mouthed my movies. I thought at the time she was just being playful. Joshing me along. But now I'm convinced that wasn't it at all. She was, and is, a bitch.

But back then, I played along with her. I continued on with my spiel. "*Showdown in Yellowknife* was the first film in my tetralogy featuring Crusher and Tex. They were up in Canada in that movie. I'm moving them down to Texas next. The public will lap up the idea."

I figured Willa'd had her fun. So I decided to tease her in return. I was absolutely, one hundred percent sure of her fidelity. So I chose a line that the two of us had played with several times before.

"Now, Mrs. Movie Critic. I have a question for you."

"Yeah, what?" she answered in that playful voice that always turned me on.

"What have you been up to today while I've been sweating over a hot plot line?"

"Oh, this, that, and the other thing." This in a sulky, provocative voice.

"Come on, Dear," I teased. "Admit it. You've got a lover."

As I told you, we'd done this bit before. And she came back at me like she'd always done. To get me horny. It always worked.

She playfully said, "You are *so* right, Rob. I have a darling, handsome lover. And I was off sucking his cock like a vacuum cleaner this morning."

I go, "Ha!"

"What do you mean, 'Ha!'?"

I thought I had her that time.

"'Sucking his cock like a vacuum cleaner.' No woman who really has a lover would say anything that corny and banal to her husband."

"You think I couldn't have myself a lover?" my wife said, acting like she was peeved.

"Of course not."

"Every married woman in Hollywood sucks off one lover or another at least once a week. Why wouldn't I?" she asked.

In my stupidity, I answered, "Because you're not like them."

"Just *how* am I 'not like them'" she retorted, sounding even more peeved. I thought she was playing her bit beautifully. All this talk had me growing hornier and hornier. So I teased her further.

"Those women are all glamorous sex goddesses. That's how you're not like them."

This was getting to be lots of fun.

"If they're 'glamorous sex goddesses,'" she replied, with real spunk in her voice, "what am I? Chopped liver?"

I liked that line, and thought I might be able to use it in a script sometime. She played her part, I thought, to perfection.

I was about to do my Tarzan act and pick her up and carry her to our bed when the doorbell rang.

"Oh, shit!" I reacted. "Let's not answer the door."

"You'd better see who it is," Willa urged. "It could be someone to rent the vacancy in 123. Or one of your important financial backers for your so-called tetralogy."

By God, she was right. The romp in the bedroom would just have to wait.

So I went to the door. And who was there but Crusher Carney.

You've seen him in my movies. He's a big guy. A man mountain. Crusher used to be a wrestler but he makes bigger bucks now as an actor. He's not too awfully bright, but I, for one, never wrote too many lines for him to remember at one time anyway. And when he muffs a line or two, it doesn't really matter. It always sounds like the part he's playing. That guy is a real treasure.

As is so often the case with the big guy, I could tell he'd been drinking. Crusher loves to drink. What a guy!

I had to invite him in.

Willa and Crusher know each other, as you might expect.

As kind of a joke, though, I said, "You remember Crusher, don't you, Dear?"

"Remember him?" she answered. "He's a little hard to miss. That bulge in his pants is his trade mark. How are you Crusher?"

"Great Mrs. Roberts," Crusher boomed. "Good to see you again."

He looked closely at Willa and said conversationally, "I see you coming and going at my apartment building in Topanga Canyon all the time. But I never get a chance to say 'Hi.' How ya' doing?"

Willa responded to that real fast, let me tell you.

"Oh, no, Crusher," she hastened to correct. "Not in Topanga Canyon. That's quite impossible. I don't even know where Topanga Canyon is."

Crusher was apologetic.

"Oh, excuse me, Ma'am. I'm a little near-sighted when I don't have on my glasses. And I hate to wear my glasses in public. Bad for the Crusher image. And when I've had a drink or two, I can kinda get confused."

I had to intercede for Crusher.

"Crusher's a fine actor, Dear. And like many members of the craft, he enjoys a relaxing drink now and then."

"To say nothing of a bit of coke, crack, weed, you name it. Like Bob here says..." Crusher tried to explain.

"Rob!" I remind him. Crusher has a hard time keeping track of names.

"Whatever," he answered. "Booze and stuff helps me relax."

Willa turned pretty cold. She just kind of clammed up. At the time, I didn't know why. I know now, of course.

I turned to Crusher.

"Crusher, you were great...simply fabulous in *Showdown at Yellowknife*. Academy award performance, I swear to God."

I noticed that Willa's attitude was growing even colder the longer Crusher was in the room. It was getting about as freezing as Yellowknife in the room.

I continued to talk to Crusher.

"You were fabulous in that scene where you crush those evil-doers that the Mounties couldn't catch. Then..."

Willa started to walk away from us, like she was going to leave the room, when the doorbell rang again.

"Shit!" I exploded. "Not again."

But I trudged over to the door. When I opened it, Tex McCall was standing there. I was afraid that at the rate we were going we'd have the whole goddam cast of my next picture in our livingroom.

"Come on in, Tex," I said, as politely as I could.

You've all seen the tabloids, so you know the cat's out of the bag. The great cowboy actor, Tex McCall of Plano, Texas actually came here to Hollywood from Brooklyn, New York. And until a few years ago his name was Irving Nussbaum. That hasn't stopped people from loving him still as Tex

McCall. Hell! Nearly everyone in this town is on his or her second or third name.

When Tex opens his mouth, he really does sound like he comes from Plano. And in that cowboy outfit he always wears, he looks like it. He's tall and rangy and walks like he has saddle sores.

But catch him off guard and every once in a while he talks like he's still that bookie back on Flatbush.

Every time he comes to our place I stand back to take a good look at him as he gets a whiff of Willa. The guy's nuts about her. Absolutely fruitcake nutso.

I called over to Willa, "Look who just came in, Honey. It's Tex."

When that lovestruck cowboy sees her, he just about comes unglued. Every time he catches sight of her he springs a huge hardon. It happens every single time. Everyone who knows to look gets a big kick out of seeing that cowboy tent his pants when he sees my wife. Willa's mood lightened up right away seeing that adoring look in Tex's eyes.

Tex was all cowboy gallantry. "Howdy, Ma'am."

"Crusher's here, too" I told Tex. "Your co-star in our last movie. And in the next three, too."

Tex said "Howdy" to Crusher. But with a lot less feeling than he'd shown towards my wife.

To decrease his bashfulness around Willa, Tex did a real dumb thing. He went over and shook Crusher's hand.

Next thing you know, he was down on his knees, writhing in pain. Everyone knows that Crusher is unaware of his own strength. He helped Tex up off the floor with a simple, "Sorry, Rex."

"Tex," was the answer.

"Whatever," was Crusher's standard reply.

The thing other than the gigantic boner Tex gets around Willa is his clumsiness. On the set, when he's making a movie, he's a well-coordinated guy. You've got to be to hop on and off horses, throw a lariat, do the fake fistfights and all. But around Willa, he really loses it.

And Willa has a little mischievous streak. I realize now that it's really a dark, mean streak. She just couldn't resist putting Tex on.

"Oh, Tex," Willa said. "What an adorable hat that is you have in your hands. Could I see it?"

There was a chair between her and Tex. And she knew it. Tex, flustered as he was, tried to walk over to her to show her the hat. And sure enough, he tripped over the chair that was in his way.

I thought it was funny at the time. But now I know it was just pure unadulterated bitchiness on Willa's part to embarrass Tex. I think his hardons inspired her somehow.

Tex got up off the floor and showed her his hat.

"Oh, yes, Tex," Willa said, taking his hat and looking at it. "It is cute. But now, if you don't mind, it's time for my afternoon nap."

"Sure, Miz Willa," he answered. "Don't want to interrupt anything. I just dropped by for a social visit. Don't want to be in the way. Come on, Crusher. Let's go down to the Go-Go Bar. I'll buy you a drink."

The invitation to the bar got Crusher going, and they were out of our place in a flash. So fast, in fact, that Tex left without his hat. It was still in Willa's hands.

Once they were gone, I sighed.

I approached Willa, beat my chest, and said, "Me Tarzan. You Jane."

I was just ready to carry her into the bedroom for a sweet fuck session that had been delayed by the visits of my two stars when – guess what happened?

The doorbell rang.

"Shit!" I moaned. "Not again. To Hell with 'em. I need to...."

"What you need to do is go to the door," Willa told me.

"I'm not going to," I insisted.

"I will, then," she snapped.

She went to the door and opened it. I heard her say:

"My goodness. Mr. Delatour. I'm a great fan of yours. Your last movie, 'The Taste of Evil' was terrific. Won't you come in?"

It was Maurice Delatour, the French actor and leading man. I'd met him from time to time around town. We're in the same business and all. And we call each other by our first names. I always thought of him as a bit of a stuffed shirt. And a ham. And I suspected him of being a fraud. But there are so many stuffed shirts, hams, and frauds in Tinsel Town that he didn't, and doesn't, particularly stand out in any of those respects.

I greeted him politely.

"Oh, Maurice. How nice to see you," I lied. "To what do we owe the pleasure?"

"Do excuse my intrusion, Rob," Maurice answered. "I'll only take up a moment of your valuable time."

"I'm not sure you've met my wife Willa before, Maurice."

"Enchanté, Madame," he said.

"Delighted," she replied.

And *that's* how it all started.

CHAPTER THREE
WILLA ON CAMERA:

You know, it still gets my goat. The way Rob found out about me and Maurice. It was my fault, though, that things turned out so messy.

I'd never paid any attention to how Rob ran that recording device he uses to write his scripts. If I'd just paid a tiny bit of attention the whole mess would not have occurred.

Anyway, here's what happened.

Maurice came to our place to rent Apartment 123. I was the one who went to the door to let him in.

We pretended we didn't know each other. I acted all flustered, like just one of his fans. He did his French "Enchanté" crap and all. We both put on quite a performance.

Rob and Maurice knew each other professionally. And like the whole Hollywood tribe they're on a first name basis. So far, so good.

"What brings you to our neck of the woods?" Rob asked.

I said, "May I get you a cup of coffee or anything, Mister...Maurice?"

He gave me that little continental bow and said, "Thank you very much...Willa. But I won't be staying long enough to enjoy your hospitality."

Then to Rob he said, "I understand that you own this building."

"No," Rob replied. "Willa here actually owns it. I manage it for her."

"I see," Maurice chimed in. "Then you are the one I need to talk to. I understand you have a ground floor apartment for rent."

"That's right," Rob responded. "Apartment 123."

"I would like to rent it" Maurice announced.

Rob looked kind of surprised.

"You would? I seem to remember that you have a mansion in Beverly Hills. I'd be glad to rent you the place downstairs, but it's rather small compared to what you have. Would you like to see it? You might find it inadequate for your needs."

Maurice explained that his lovely home in Beverly Hills was some distance from the Olympic Studios where he works in Hollywood. And that there were many occasions when it would be convenient to have a pied-à-terre (his expression) in Hollywood where he could relax after a day at the studio, particularly when rush hour traffic would be a bother.

I responded enthusiastically to Maurice's explanation. Rob answered in a businesslike way, saying he would be honored to have a talented thespian like Maurice as a tenant. He had the rental agreement forms in another room and went off to get them, leaving Maurice and me alone in the livingroom.

As soon as Rob was out of the room, I said:

"You can drop the French accent now, Barney. I'd like you to be your other self during this delicious moment when we're stealing a little love together right under Rob's nose."

I sidled up to him and rubbed his crotch until he got hard as a rock.

Maurice took me in his arms and treated me to one of those kisses for which he's so justly famous as Maurice Delatour the great French lover while slipping a hand under my skirt and rubbing my koozie. I didn't mind him slipping from role to role. It was a kick exchanging feelie probes with Rob in the next room.

My lover said "When I get possession of that apartment downstairs, we can enjoy each other's embraces like this much more often. And without all these clothes on."

I said, "That *love (click)* nest of yours, apartment 206 at Eleven Topanga Canyon Boulevard is so far away. And Crusher Carney apparently lives in that building. Just a little while ago he claimed he saw me coming and going from there. Even so, I'll risk going there one more time to be in your arms tonight."

"Did Crusher say that when Rob was around?"

"Yeah. But old Rob didn't get it at all. I'd *hate (click)* for him to get wind of what we're doing."

We stopped feeling each other up not a moment too soon. Because just then Rob came bursting back into the room with the legal forms.

He announced, "Here's the paperwork. Let's see. Do you want the place month-to-month or on a year's lease?"

Maurice got his French accent back and answered, "At least a year, Rob."

With that he gave me a wink Rob couldn't see because he was filling out the forms.

The two men signed the papers and Maurice wrote a check. With that finished, Maurice headed for the door fast.

Rob took the lease and the check off to the other room.

When Rob came back into the room Maurice was gone.

Now I had to prepare some way to get out of the apartment that evening.

"Oh, Rob," I said. "You *do* remember I'm taking my mom out tonight to Pantages to see *The Doll House*, don't you?"

I knew how Rob hated stage plays. Movies are his idea of where acting occurs. And he can't stand my mother. He has that male mother-in-law phobia that obsesses so many guys. So, as always, I knew I could get away to my 'tryst' scot-free.

"Go on," Rob said jovially. "Give the old bat my regards. And enjoy the play, if you can."

In about a half hour I was out of the apartment on my way to Topanga Canyon for the 'tryst.'

It felt so naughty, so daring, and...so exciting.

CHAPTER FOUR
ROB ON CAMERA:

Willa was off to see that old bat, her mother. And I could get back to work. With all the ins and outs of zanies who had come streaming into our place I hadn't managed to get much work done. Now I figured I could get in a few hours more of script composing.

I rewound my tape a bit to gather the way my mind had been working when I cut it off last.

I started it up. "Love!" But at first I couldn't make out what I was hearing. It was Willa's voice, not mine.

What I heard Willa saying was:

"Nest of yours, apartment 206 at Eleven Topanga Canyon Boulevard is so far away. And Crusher Carney apparently lives in that building. Just a little while ago he claimed he saw me coming and going from there. Even so, I'll risk going there one more time to be in your arms tonight."

I switched it off. Yep, it was Willa's voice all right. How the Hell did it get onto my tape? She had to have been in this room and said 'Love' and turned it on by mistake. I replayed it to make sure I'd heard right. I couldn't believe my ears.

I picked up from there and heard a high pitched male voice. But not one I recognized at all. Here's what I heard.

"Did Crusher say that when Rob was around?"

That was it. Pretty much a standard Southern California accent. Somewhat high pitched. Like a tenor. Maybe a tad higher.

Who the Hell could it be? Local accent. High pitched voice. I played it over several times and couldn't get a clue.

Then I picked it up from where I had left off. It was Willa again. Here. I'll play it for you.

"Yeah. But old Rob didn't get it at all. I'd hate..."

And it clicked off right there.

Who was that guy? It sounded a little like Tex. But the accent wasn't Texas or Brooklyn. And I'd never heard Tex go falsetto. Not even that time the horse kicked him in the nuts. But still...

I just couldn't figure out who the guy was. But I *did* know one thing. My wife would be in his arms that very evening. What a fool I had been. Off to take her mother to a play at Pantages, huh?

I was stewing in my own juices. Mad as Hell. And just then the goddam doorbell rang.

I answered it and guess who was standing there? My number one suspect, that's who. Tex McCall.

"Uh, hi, Rob," he said, kind of embarrassed. "I rushed out of here without my Stetson. I guess it's over there on the couch."

"You son of a bitch!" I shouted. "Go get your goddam hat. And shove it up your fucking ass."

Tex seemed kind of surprised at my outburst. But he did step lively into the room, picked up his hat, and began to scurry back towards the door.

I railed at him as he sidled past me.

"Don't forget your hat when you get to Eleven Topanga Canyon Boulevard. Willa's probably waiting for you there in Apartment 206. Go to her. If *you're* what she wants, you can have her. Go fuck her until she shits her pants."

"Fuck...shit...what?"

As angry as I was, I still paid careful attention to his voice. He was rattled, so probably speaking in his real accent. Did I hear Texas? Did I hear Brooklyn? Did I hear Southern California? Did his voice sound a higher range than I was used to for him?

I couldn't tell. All I knew was that my wife had betrayed me and planned to betray me again in the arms of her unknown lover.

I swore I would get her for that. Willa would not escape my

vengeance.

CHAPTER FIVE
WILLA ON CAMERA:

I got to the love nest in Topanga Canyon before Maurice. I was happy that this would be our last time there. The place is a little on the tacky side. It's a studio apartment. One of those jobbies with a combination livingroom-bedroom that greets you when you enter. There's a kitchenette with a pass-through counter between it and the bedroom-livingroom. And, naturally, there's a bathroom. No tub. Only a shower, wash basin, and toilet. The furnishings are like early garage. A king-size bed. That was essential. A coffee table's next to the bed. There's a kind of beat-up dresser with a mirror over it and a little radio on top. A couple of chairs, two standing lamps... You get the picture. Not too romantic. And I was a little uneasy because I was somewhat spooked by Crusher's remark that he'd seen me around the building.

I freshened up and got ready to receive my lover.

I opened the top drawer of the dresser, where Maurice kept several tubes of KY Jelly. I took one out and put it on the coffee table next to the bed.

Then I took off my clothes and went into the bathroom. I got in the shower to wash up.

When I got out of the shower, dried off, and got my clothes back on, I didn't have to wait long for Maurice to arrive.

He breezed through the door with a jaunty smile on his lips and a paper bag in his hands.

"Ah," he said in his French accent. "My little flower awaits the coming of her lover bee. But she is over-dressed. A flower must be open to the caresses of her lover bee."

It was pretty corny. But I loved it. The games we played in our lovemaking really turned me on back then.

"What has my lover bee brought in the pretty brown bag?" I asked.

"The distillation of the sugar cane," he smiled.

"Oh, goody. Rum," I exclaimed.

Out of the bag he brought a bottle of Bacardi and a bottle of daiquiri mix.

"I have a little something here to enliven the party," he buzzed.

"While I prepare a little libation," he continued. "Feel free to make yourself more comfortable. When I get our daiquiris mixed, we can begin our little game."

"Sounds good," I replied in as sexy a voice as I could manage.

"Get yourself out there in the kitchen to mix the drinks, and after that, we'll play Act One."

Maurice took the rum and the mix into the kitchenette and began to fix the drinks.

He came back into the bedroom/livingroom with the cocktails.

I kissed him on the mouth, and as our tongues mated I did something I really love doing. I rubbed his cock through his pants. He reciprocated by rubbing my tits. We were both fully aroused. And, at that point, I enjoy calling a recess.

"I need a drink," I announced.

Maurice filled our glasses. We both took pretty healthy swigs of our drinks.

"Your feet," my lover said. "I adore those sexy feet of yours. May I?"

I knew what "May I" meant. I laid my drink on the coffee table and spread myself out on the bed. Maurice settled himself at the foot of the bed and began caressing my feet. I told you Maurice is a foot man, didn't I? He was certainly a novelty in my love life.

He began massaging my feet with a deft touch. It was a turn-on for him. It did very little for me sexually, but it *did* feel very nice anyway. I knew the next step. It was why I had washed my feet before his arrival.

He began to suck my toes, one at a time. If you've never had your toes sucked you can't imagine the feeling. He would suck my pinky. Then he'd slip his tongue between the pinkie and the next toe and tongued that space with soft, slow ins and outs. Then, one by one, he continued to the big toe. And he sucked that one with a passion.

Maurice finished off one foot and proceeded on to the next with the same relish he had lavished on the other

When he'd finished off my feet, he proceeded to nibble at my legs until he got up to the inside of my thighs. I got really tingly there. Next, his tongue pounced down onto my twat, slurping at the lips like a kitten would. Next, he licked my clit until it got to throbbing. He sucked the little button until I came full force. Then we proceeded to make love with nearly missionary matrimonial practices for a while. He got to pumping, then, harder and harder until we both came in a sudden wild burst.

We were both out of breath by then. Maurice hoisted himself up beside me, held me in his arms, and we sighed with contentment at each other.

After a brief rest, it was time for another drink.

We finished off the daiquiris in our glasses and Maurice refilled them. I was really feeling no pain by then.

"I guess that's the end of Act One," I decided.

Each time we both reached our simultaneous orgasms it was the end of an act in the love dramas we produced.

"How many acts do you think tonight's drama will have?" Maurice asked.

As always, I replied. "The more the better."

I can give the guy this. Just because we'd done Act One, it didn't mean he was going to give up.

Act Two soon followed. And, by golly, we even managed to get through Act Three. We were both kind of worn out by then.

My God how that man could fuck, suck, and massage.

I needed another drink.

As exhausted as we were, we proceeded on to Act Four, Act Five, and then I lost count because we kept punctuating our fucking and sucking with daiquiris and both passed out in a drunken stupor.

CHAPTER SIX
WILLA ON CAMERA:

After what I thought must have been a blackout of a couple of hours I awoke with the mother of all headaches. The bursting headache was bad enough. But the rumblings in my stomach took precedence. How much of that rum had we downed?

The liquor bottle was sitting on the pass-through counter to the kitchenette. I tried to focus my blurry eyes on it. I couldn't swear to it, but it looked like the two of us had killed the whole damned bottle.

Jesus! My head! My stomach! Oops!

I made a dash for the bathroom. Things were coming back up. Probably a good thing.

I kneeled down next to the toilet and heaved and heaved. Nasty stuff. Ugh! But good to get rid of it before it made me even sicker than I already felt.

When I'd emptied my stomach, and then retched for another ten minutes or so, I staggered back into the livingroom-bedroom. Barney was tossing around in his sleep. He was definitely Barney, not Maurice. His fans certainly would not have recognized him as the suave continental leading man they adored. And since I'd last seen him he'd grown a dark stubble on his face.

I stumbled over to the bed and poked him.

"Hey, Barney! Wake up!"

He stirred, tried to sit up, grabbed his head, moaned, eased back down onto his pillow and said, "Go away!"

I wasn't going to let him off that easy. I poked him in the ribs. And it was not a gentle poke.

"Come on, Barney," I urged. "Wake up! I need an Alka-seltzer or Pepto-Bismol or an aspirin or...Oh, for God's sake, Barney. Where do you keep stuff to handle a hangover?"

He just grunted and burrowed his face deeper into his pillow.

So I grabbed him by his feet and started to drag him towards the end of the bed. If that didn't rouse him, I was prepared grab his balls and squeeze hard. I was damned if I was going to suffer alone in silence.

Luckily for him the yank on his feet did the trick.

"What the Hell...?" he growled. Not his cute little Frenchified growl but more like that of an awakening souse.

"Aspirin, Barney. Or Pepto..."

"Oops!" he said, and made a beeline for the bathroom. He was up now. And upchucking the remnants of the daiquiris from his belly.

When he finally came back into the room he was an ashen color that was less than attractive.

We sat down next to each other on the side of the bed, holding our throbbing heads.

"Man!" He exclaimed. "Did we ever tie one on!"

"What do you have in this dump for a hangover, Sport?" I asked.

He tried to shake his head, and suddenly thought better of it.

"I wish I had something," he moaned. "I could use a little anything myself. Jesus! My head!"

I was really miffed.

"You dumbass fucking bastard!" I exploded, despite my pounding head. "You load us up with enough rum to sink Cuba and don't even have the sense to put any..."

"Shut the fuck up!" he interrupted. "You're just making my headache worse."

I could see this was getting us nowhere fast. So I decided to try to sound more civil.

"How long do you think we passed out here?" I asked.

"Probably a couple of hours," he said, and reached over to the coffee table for his watch.

He squinted at his watch-face. He was having a hard time focusing on it. I knew how he felt. My vision was pretty blurry too.

"Goddam it!" He shouted. Then he held his head. Speaking that loud was a bad idea in the shape we were in.

"What?" I inquired.

"It's six o'clock."

I couldn't process that.

"No, Barney. That can't be. I'm sure we were on our second drink around seven. It must be closer to ten or ten-thirty. And time for me to get back home. Rob thinks I've been to the theater with my mother."

"Think again, Sugar Plum," he said, real snide like. "I'm not talking six at night. It's six in the morning."

It couldn't be! He had to be making a ghastly joke. And I was in no mood for practical jokes. Maybe his watch was wrong.

"Get up and go over to the dresser, Barney and turn on the goddam radio," I ordered him. "Let's see if we can't get a little reality going here."

Barney stood up with a loud groan. Standing there nude, hung over, stubble faced, and unable to stand erect, he was a sorry sight. But then nothing was likely to look good to me until I could get some relief from that pulsating hangover.

He clicked on the radio.

A voice that was too cheery by far came blaring out of the contraption.

"Good morning, Angelinos. It's six-ten. Traffic on the Harbor Freeway..."

Maurice clicked it off. With one voice we moaned, "Holy fucking shit!"

Maurice looked very distraught.

He said, "Jesus Christ! What a disaster."

I told him that it was more of a disaster for me than for him.

"Why's that?" he asked.

"Because I'm the one who's married," I explained.

"You aren't the only one," he shot back.

The bastard! He had told me he was a bachelor.

"Of course I told you I'm a bachelor. I never tell the women I fuck that I'm married. What would *that* do to my sex life?"

So we were both in the same pickle. What would I tell Rob? What would that rotten, no good bastard I'd been fucking and sucking tell his wife?

I would have probably got into a fight with him about his duplicity, but we suddenly grew deathly silent. There was a rustle at the door. Someone was fooling around outside with the doorknob.

What to do?

Barney and I looked at each other with panic in our eyes. Then, together, we uttered the same advice.

"Hide!"

I bounded out of bed and achieved the sanctity of the bathroom in practically one leap.

Barney slid down under the covers and pulled them over his head.

The door to the apartment opened. I realized that my lover had not re-set the lock when he came in. We'd left the place unlocked. I peeked around the bathroom door to try to get a glimpse of who the intruder was. And who did I see come staggering in?

Crusher Carney!

Crusher looked at the bed and was aware that there was a figure huddled under the covers. He addressed the figure.

"Oh, hi, Maisie," he slurred. "It's me. I'm home. I just stopped on my way here to have a few drinks with the boys at the Sumo Grill down on Sunset Boulevard. But I'm back now, and ready for a little loving."

He stood by one of the chairs. Not the one where Barney's clothes were folded. The other one. And he kind of wobbled and teetered there.

"I'll be with you in a moment, Honey Bunch," Crusher mumbled. "Soon's I get outta these clothes."

Through the crack in the door, I had a perfect view of him. He sat down on the chair and, with some difficulty, got his shoes and socks off. Then he stood and got the rest of his clothes off. He just left his clothes piled on the floor next to the chair.

Crusher was a big, strong, muscular guy with an impressive build. And hung! God, how that man was hung. A cock that could fit on a horse!

In his nude state, Crusher crawled into bed with my former lover. Maurice (I wanted to think of him more as Maurice than Barney under the circumstances) sidled away from him.

"Aw, come on, Maisie," Crusher urged. "Don't be that way. I'm in the mood for looove!"

I watched in horror, fascination, and glee as Crusher put his massive arms around little Maurice and pulled him close. I could see Maurice trembling. He was facing away from Crusher, so they were spooned together.

"Come, Honey Bunch," Crusher crooned. "You know you love it. And so do I."

With that, Maurice let out a scream that nearly raised the roof. I had the hardest time stifling my laughter.

Crusher was fucking Maurice in the ass. The little faux Frenchman was getting cornholed by the biggest dong in Hollywood.

"I love it when you scream with delight," Crusher murmured as he rhythmically rammed that cock up my former lover's ass.

At first I was horrified by what was happening.

But you know what I suddenly realized? Maurice wasn't fighting Crusher off. From the sound of his moans, he was actually enjoying being cornholed by the Crusher. Damn!

When Crusher had finished with Maurice, he sweet-talked him.

"Maisie. You were really great this morning."

Crusher turned his back on Maurice, still mumbling loving thoughts. Maurice sneaked one leg out of the bed, then the other. He very quietly got the rest of his body out from under the covers and then out of bed entirely.

"That's okay," Crusher said. "You go to the bathroom first, Dear. When you're through, I've gotta go pee, too."

Maurice eyed his clothes that were folded on the chair. He clearly wanted to get to them, get them on, and get out.

Unfortunately, Crusher was facing that chair. Presumably with his eyes closed. I could see that Maurice was getting ready to chance it. The odds were that Crusher would keep his eyes closed. Maybe he would even have fallen asleep.

Maurice tiptoed toward the chair. He was absolutely silent in his stealth.

He got safely to the chair and was ready to grab his clothes when Crusher sat upright in bed looking directly at Maurice.

"Maisie," he said. "A man got into our room. And he's nude. You stay in the bathroom until I've taken care of the dude. Don't worry. I won't let him harm you."

I thought Maurice would faint.

Crusher leapt out of bed, towering over Maurice.

"Okay, you," he threatened. "Who the Hell are you and what are you doing in our place?"

Maurice had to think fast.

"Oh, Sir," Maurice said. "I just happened in by mistake. I thought this was my home on Mulholland Drive. I must have taken a wrong turn on the road."

Fortunately Crusher, drunk, bleary-eyed, and without his glasses did not recognize Maurice.

"Took the wrong turn, did you?" Crusher questioned. Then, he caught sight of Maurice's clothes neatly folded on the chair.

"What's them?" he asked, somewhat ungrammatically.

"My clothes," Maurice answered, stating the obvious.

"Crusher will teach the Mulholland intruder a lesson he will never forget," Crusher told him. He picked up Maurice's clothes, and with admirable dispatch threw them out the window and into the street below.

"Why did you do that?" Maurice whimpered.

"To teach you a lesson. That's what," Crusher growled. "Now get the Hell out of my place."

Maurice could not leave the room in his nude state. But he didn't want to anger Crusher any further. So he walked toward the door.

Crusher staggered over to the bathroom door I was hiding behind.

"It's all right to come out now, Maisie," Crusher called out. "The pervert's gone."

He pulled the door open and there I was facing him. Both of us nude as Greek statues. I was face to face with that grand, exciting cock.

At the same time, Maurice took refuge in the closet next to the front door and slammed the closet door behind him.

"Hear that, Sweetie?" Crusher said to me. "The bastard's left. Let's get back in bed and have ourselves another party."

The big dolt didn't take time to look at me carefully enough to see that I was not his Maisie. I figured I'd better play the part of Maisie anyway. At that point, I figured why not go with the flow. What the Hell? The man had invited me to a party. It just might be a lot of fun.

This time it was Maurice who was peeking from behind a door. And Crusher had rammed that horse pizzle up my cunt until I thought it would come out my mouth.

Crusher's technique was a million times less sophisticated than that of the man watching us through the crack in the closet door. But I wouldn't have missed the experience for the world. I guess you could say I was "fulfilled."

So Crusher and I had ourselves one Hell of a time. And it kind of pleased me knowing Maurice was watching us. The thought occurred to me that Maurice hadn't put up any more resistance than I was showing. What a hoot! We both clearly loved it.

After Crusher had done me royally, he took my head into his massive hands and brought my face up to his for a kiss. But before he could manage the kiss, he got a good look at me.

"Jesus!" he exclaimed. "You're not Maisie. You're Rob Roberts' wife!"

I had to think fast. And I was pretty sure I could think faster than this big lunk who had just had his way with me. (Sigh!)

"No, no," I said in my best attempt at a Chinese accent. "Me not wifee of no Rob. Me Chung-chug Fat. Me the laundry lady."

"Laundry lady?" Crusher questioned, showing massive confusion. "You mean I've been humping the Chinese laundry lady?"

"Oh, you humpee real good," I complemented him, not dishonestly. "But now me must get to laundly chop-chop."

"Sorry," Crusher apologized. "Without my glasses I don't see so good."

I thought this would be a good opportunity to get Maurice out of the place safely. He didn't deserve my help, but I thought that if we could both get away, things would certainly be less complicated.

"Ah, so, Mister," I said. "Funny thing happen. My husband, Ding-A-Ling get stuck in closet. Ding-A-Ling and me go away cop-chop now. Come out of closet Ding-A-Ling."

Maurice kind of slithered out of the closet. Crusher took a half-hearted look at him and accepted my word.

"Me put on clothes now," I said.

Maurice went over to the window to take a look at the clothes Crusher had thrown out.

"Yeah, Hung-chug Fat," he said in a poor accent for a Chinese. But at least he didn't put on his phony French accent. "You get dressed, go downstairs and get my clothes and bring them up here. Then we chop-chop lickety-splitee."

"Good idea, Ding-A-Ling," I agreed.

Maurice looked out the window.

"Oh my God," he said. "My clothes aren't down there any more. The trash collectors must have come by and picked them up."

"I've gotta get me some shut-eye," Crusher said, losing interest in the Chinese couple who had appeared in what he thought was his apartment.

And with that, he shuffled off to dreamland and began snoring immediately.

I quickly slipped on my clothes.

Maurice took the only option open to him and put on Crusher's clothes. They fit him like a tent. He could hardly move they enveloped him so.

We were no sooner dressed and ready to escape out into the wilds of Topanga Canyon than there was a knock on the door.

"Knock, knock."

"Who's there?" asked Maurice.

"Rob," came the answer.

"Rob who?" Maurice asked foolishly.

"Rob, me, you bastard!" Rob said, pulling the door open.

Damn! Obviously Crusher had not managed to re-set the little doodad in the doorknob when he came in. It was just like my dingaling lover. The door had remained unlocked the whole time.

When I recognized who it was, I ran back to the bed and hid under the covers.

"Oh, hello Rob," Maurice said in his most urbane manner. "Things are not at all what they appear to be. I am completely innocent of what you may be thinking. As far as what your wife and Crusher are doing over there in bed, I leave up to your imagination."

Crusher woke up when Rob entered. And my dive under the covers seemed not to confuse him too much.

Rob was clearly surprised.

He pushed Maurice aside as if he were inconsequential.

"Shut up, Maurice," he snarled. "I'll deal with you later."

"Crusher!" Rob shouted. "What are you doing in bed with my wife?"

Crusher was all friendliness and smiles.

"Oh, hi, Rob. Yeah. At first I thought she was your wife too. Turns out she's a Chinese laundress. I can't remember her name."

"What are you doing here in the first place?" Rob asked Crusher.

"I live here," Crusher said amiably. "This apartment 306 is where Maisie and me live."

Then he thought for a moment.

"But where's Maisie?"

Rob was willing to cut Crusher the slack he deserved.

"This is *not* apartment 306, Crusher. It's *two*-o-six. You stumbled into the wrong place."

"Golly, I didn't know," Crusher said. "Sorry. I'd better get upstairs. Maisie'll be worried about me. But, I'll tell you one thing, Rob. That Chinese laundress is Hell on wheels in bed."

With that he exited in all his nudity and walked slowly up the stairs to his own place.

He was barely out the door when Tex came bursting in.

"Hi, there, Little Lady," Tex drawled, unaware at first that Rob and Maurice were in the room with me. "Rob tells me you're waiting for me. Sorry I couldn't get away from my wife until now."

"Sorry, Tex," Rob explained. "Willa wasn't waiting for you after all."

"Oh," Tex replied, disappointed. "Then I reckon I might as well go back to my wife."

"You might as well," Rob said evenly.

Tex turned tail and ambled off with his standard Western gait.

"I believe I will take my leave as well," Maurice said with over-exaggerated dignity.

"I'll be seeing you later, Maurice," Rob said, a threatening tone showing through his measured speech.

As Maurice proceeded out the door, he couldn't resist throwing out an exit line.

He went, "All I can say is, she wasn't worth it."

That rat!

CHAPTER SEVEN
HAROLD ON CAMERA:

My name is Harold Tremaine. And, over at Olympic Studios, I'm a best boy.

Do you know what that means? It's a technical movie studio title that refers to the chief assistant to the gaffer. To hold down the job, a guy's got to be a skilled electrician. Which I am.

But, why I'm on camera now is to explain that I'm Maurice Delatour's best friend. Even though at the moment Maurice doesn't seem to think so.

As good a friend as I am of Maurice, I'm an even better friend of his wife Charlene. I'm really crazy about her. As a matter of fact, if I weren't so hot for her, I'd drop old Maurice in a jiffy

Maurice Delatour's wife, Charlene, is one nifty babe. She's beautiful, gentle, not too bright, and a great fuck. What more could anyone ask of a woman? And in addition to those fine qualities, on this particular night, she was worried. Which meant she needed comforting. And something I really love to do is comfort Charlene.

This time I want to tell you about, Maurice was missing from action. That is, he'd told Charlene he was going to be working late at the studio. According to what he'd explained to her, there was a complicated scene in the movie they were shooting, *Love on the Left Bank*, that could keep him at Olympic until possibly even midnight. Charlene was used to that. It happened all the time.

I knew Maurice was going to be out late. He always brags to me about the dolls he's wooing. So I know when he's going to be out tomcatting. And, of course, whenever I know he's going to be away from home, which is often, I'm at his house fucking his wife.

I've fucked quite a few wives of the stars at Olympic Studios. And that's where I come in. I book myself as the 'best boy to lovelorn actors' wives as 'best boy' in a different sense.

This night I want to tell you about, I was at the Delatour mansion in Beverly Hills. Charlene and I were in the master bedroom having ourselves a time. She loves to get her cunt lapped. And I'm probably the best muff diver in Hollywood. She returns the favor with a little sucking trick she does on my peckerhead. It's quite a treat for both of us. That, of course, is in addition to good old-fashioned fucking.

I was at Maurice's place, in Maurice's bed, and enjoying Maurice's wife. But, like with all the other wives I service, I had an ear open for hubby coming home. When the front door opens, I'm outta bed, into my clothes, and out the back door in a jiffy, while wifey-poo slips into a negligee and goes to the front of the house to greet Mr. Cuckold with kisses and whatever else will hold him until I make my clean getaway.

Like I said, Charlene and I were having ourselves a royal old time. I was real aware of the time. I can always tell when it's eleven o'clock. I go on special alert at eleven. The husbands generally like to finish off their little side-pieces in time to get home to their waiting wives between eleven and twelve.

The sport the Lotharios' wives and I have in bed between eleven and midnight is often pretty frantic. A real sense of excitement gets to brewing when we know the front door could be swinging open at any second. That hour is my favorite in the whole day.

On the night I'm telling you about, when the clock down the hall chimed midnight, Charlene began to fret.

She told me, "Harold, I'm worried. Maurice is always home by Midnight when there's a late shoot at the studio."

"I wouldn't worry yet, Babe," I soothed her. "I happen to know that the scene they're trying to perfect is extremely tricky. The leading man is about to try to do *this* to Antoinette."

I demonstrated rather than described by running my tongue clean up into her twat..

When Charlene caught her breath, she asked, "And then what?"

"Then what, what?" I ask.

"The leading man is about to do 'that.' Then what?" she wanted to know.

"Oh! Then Maurice comes charging into the sewers of Paris," I explained. "And since the flick's supposed to be rated "G" it has to be kept clean. But it keeps looking too much like a pornflick with what the guy's really doing... It's really too technical to explain. Trust me, Charlene. It's very complicated and it could take them until well past midnight to get it right. So let's just enjoy ourselves and forget it."

She agreed. And I got a deep-throat from her that she'd been practicing on me. When it got to one in the morning, I just could no longer keep Charlene from fretting. She insisted we get out of bed and go into the livingroom to await the return of my missing best friend.

So we were sitting there on the sofa in that front room, and I was giving the lady loving consolation by gently massaging her tits. We heard a car pull up to the curb outside.

"It sounds like a car pulling up at the curb outside, Harold," Charlene observed. "Would you go check? It might be Maurice."

I looked out the window.

"No, Charlene," I told her. "It's just a fat lady getting out of a taxi. She's paying the driver. Now she's heading for the house across the street."

"It's that slut Hilda De Vrees," Charlene commented.

I rushed back to the sofa so I could continue to comfort her.

"Oh, Harold," she said after a little while. "I'm so worried. I'm afraid something terrible has happened to Maurice...which...You're his best friend, Harold...Can't you do something?"

Couldn't I do something? I'd called the cops to tell them Maurice was late getting home. They weren't very interested. I'd called a couple of hospitals. They didn't have any information. I even called the morgue. Maurice hadn't registered in there either. How could I show my concern for my best friend beyond that?

As time wore on, Charlene grew more agitated about her husband.

"Surely there's something more you could do," she urged.

I could tell I wasn't going to get any more action with her for a while. I wasn't up to it anyway. And she was now obsessed with the missing phony Frenchman.

I had an idea.

"I have a friend who's a cop," I said. "I could call him."

"But you said the police weren't interested when you called them before," Charlene noted.

"That's right," I answered. "But Lieutenant Mertz, my buddy, might take a personal interest in the matter. The sergeant I talked to on the phone a while ago was just acting routinely. He didn't take any personal interest. My friend Mertz might."

"Well, call your lieutenant friend if you think it might do some good." Charlene agreed.

I called Mertz at his home. I woke him from his sleep. At first he sounded kinda grouchy. But when I told him a big movie star was missing he got real interested. I told him where I was and he said he'd be right over.

Charlene was very grateful.

"Oh, Harold," she enthused. "You are such a comfort. And such a good friend of Maurice's. He was just mentioning you to me a couple of days ago. He was saying, 'Harold Tremaine may be a few scenes short of a full script, but he's a fair friend."

"Touching," I said.

We sat there waiting for Mertz to come. And like I said, there was no sense trying to get any action going again with Charlene.

A police car pulled up outside before long. And I saw it was my friend Lieutenant Mertz getting out. When he got to the front door, I was there to let him in. As he entered he said to me, "I hope this is a juicy one, Harold. I appreciate you calling me."

"What are friends for?" I retorted.

Charlene stood up to welcome him. She extended her hand.

"Widow Delatour," Mertz said gallantly. "Pleased to meet you."

Poor Charlene was taken aback.

"Widow?" she questioned. "You mean you've found...?"

Mertz smiled deferentially.

"Aw, no, Ma'am. Just wishful thinking. I've just got started on the case. No bodies...yet."

Charlene seemed relieved.

Lt. Mertz went on to explain.

"Think nothing of it, Ma'am. I've been looking for a good homicide case for years. We've had some beauts here in L.A. Now take the O.J. Simpson case. We lost that one. And then there was the Black Dahlia. Never solved to my satisfaction. I wasn't on the force back then. But Maurice Delatour.

Famous French actor. The great lover. Wow! What I wouldn't do to crack *this* case."

I could tell Charlene was growing uncomfortable with the direction Mertz was taking.

But Mertz kept right on rhapsodizing.

"I always thought Fate would deal me a straight flush eventually. Maurice Delatour. Here today, snuffed tomorrow. Maybe we'll call it the Case of the Croaked Frog. How does *that* grab you?"

It grabbed me fine, but seemed to distress Charlene. I thought perhaps she needed some comforting in the bedroom. I was about to suggest exactly that when Mertz began questioning her.

"Harold here says your husband hasn't been seen since yesterday afternoon. Famous person. *World* famous. Heart-throb of millions of broads. Recognizable wherever he goes. Women sit in the movie houses, watch him on the screen, and practically come right there. So what we seem to have here is a clear case of murder."

I thought that sounded swell. But Charlene got even more shook up than before.

"Just a few simple questions, Ma'am," Mertz continued. "I just want the facts."

Charlene braced herself to do her duty to the law.

"Does your husband happen to be a dope fiend? Any drugs?" Mertz asked.

"He takes Viagra regularly for his heart condition." Charlene volunteered.

"Just the facts, Ma'am. Anything else? Heroin? Coke?"

"He always liked rum and coke. But more often daiquiris," Charlene said helpfully.

Mertz jotted that down.

"Hmmm. Rum. Coke. Daiquiris. How do you spell daiquiri? Never mind. This'll do. Now, tell me, Ma'am. Did your husband consort with mafia types? Kidnappers? Hit men?"

"Only on the set," Charlene stated.

That elated Mertz.

"'On the set.' Now we're getting somewhere." Mertz said.

"Now, Mrs. Delatour. Can you describe your husband's other bad habits?"

"Other...?"

"You know. Is he a transvestite? Or a pederast? That kind

of thing?" Mertz pressed.

"Transvestite?" she asked, perplexed at where Mertz was leading.

"You know," Mertz explained. "Did he prance around dressed up in your clothes. Did he go out in drag looking for other men to get his jollies with?"

"Really!" Charlene objected.

"Or, like I say," Mertz pressed on enthusiastically. "Might he be a pederast? Did he like to do naughty things like diddle little boys? A lot of entertainers are into that. Can't keep their hands off those little wee-wees. Know what I mean. We have a hard time nabbing them, but..."

"My husband did not, I mean does not diddle little boys," Charlene huffed.

As far as I knew that was true. But I didn't feel a need to put my two cents in.

Just then the doorbell rang.

"Maybe that's Maurice now," Charlene hoped.

"I'll get it," I volunteered.

I got to the door and a man from the waste management company was standing there. He was holding a pile of clothes.

"Yes?" I inquired.

"Is this the home of Maurice Delatour?"

I acknowledged it was.

"Here's Mr. Delatour's clothes," the guy told me, extending the package.

"His clothes? What makes you think those are his clothes?"

"'Cause his wallet with all his I.D.'s in it. Keys too. They probably fit this here door."

"Where were these found?"

"Trash pickup at Eleven Topanga Canyon Boulevard" the man explained.

"What were they doing there?"

"Laying in a heap I guess," the man shrugged. "I wasn't there. My job's just to deliver 'em and get a receipt."

I signed for the clothes, brought them into the living room, and presented them to Lt. Mertz.

"Aha!" Mertz exclaimed. "Another break in the case. Where did you say they were found?"

"Eleven Topanga Canyon Boulevard. In a heap."

"If those are his clothes," Mertz asked. "Where's Delatour's body?"

Neither Charlene or I had an answer to that crucial question.

"Oh, boy!" Mertz exulted. "What a break! If these are his clothes, Delatour has to be nude. A nude corpse! Can a corpse have a hardon? That would make a terrific story. The broads will love it. The press will eat this up. I'll be famous...famous!"

I could see why my policeman friend was so happy. I kind of dug the situation myself.

Mertz gloated on.

"Hot diggity dog! Do we ever have a case on our hands. The Topanga Canyon Strangler. Nude corpse of Hollywood's greatest lover, complete with boner."

I was getting into it with him. But poor Charlene just seemed to become more dismayed.

"I can see the headlines now," Mertz went on. "'Mertz Cracks Case of Croaked Frog.' Maybe I'll write a book. 'How I solved Hollywood's Greatest Murder Mystery.' By Lieutenant Mergatroid Mertz, LAPD. As told to... Who's gonna write the book I'm gonna write?"

I bought into that one.

"Don't worry about it, Mertz. Hack writers are a dime a dozen in this town. I'll get you one. I'll be your agent. You'll be famous...and I'll be rich."

"Gee! That sounds great, Harold," Mertz exulted. "Now I'm gonna look through the pockets of these here pants for clues. Let's see. One handkerchief, not used. Wallet, driver's license, credit cards, two hundred fifty three dollars in cash, a set of car keys, two sets of house keys..."

Charlene challenged that.

"Two sets?"

"Anything suspicious in that?" the lieutenant asked.

Charlene said she was only aware of Maurice having one set of keys.

Mertz jotted down a note.

"A significant clue."

He continued with a search of the pockets.

"Two condoms."

Charlene was puzzled again.

"Condoms? I don't understand."

Lt. Mertz tried to help.

"They're called rubbers, Ma'am. They're for protection. You see, when he's nailing all them starlets, he don't wanna..."

"Please, Lieutenant," Charlene said. "I don't really want to hear any more."

"O.K.," Mertz said. "No problem."

All that apparently still remained in the pockets was some loose change. Mertz counted it out. Seventy-three cents.

"Have you come to any conclusions?" I asked.

"Yes, I have, Harold," my policeman friend told me. "On the basis of my findings so far, I'd say we have a definite high-profile murder case on our hands. Most likely death by strangulation. But we'll need a forensic report to verify that."

I asked, naively, if the police could make a forensic report without a body.

Mertz proudly replied, "You'd be surprised what we can write a forensic report on."

Charlene let out a little scream.

"Someone's breaking into the house, Lieutenant!"

Mertz drew his pistol and pointed it at the door.

"Hold up your hands or I'll shoot!" he barked.

And who should come on in, dressed in clothes about ten sizes too big for him, and his hands in the air, but my best friend.

Maurice piped up, "Don't shoot! Don't shoot!"

Charlene was ecstatic. "Maurice, it's you! Alive!"

Mertz muttered, "Damn!"

Under my breath I echoed the same thought.

Maurice looked at me and said, "There's a taxi outside waiting for a fare. Pay him, will you, Harold?"

I went out and paid, then hustled right back in to get the scoop on what had happened. Charlene asked, with loving concern, "Where have you been, Maurice?"

Mertz and I were like echoes, but with less loving concern.

"Yeah. Where have you been?"

"To Las Vegas," Maurice answered confidently.

Charlene thought the answer strange.

"To Las Vegas? In those clothes? What strange attire for Las Vegas, Dear."

Maurice, accomplished actor that he is, decided to take the high road.

"Wait just one moment here, everyone. Before I answer one more question, I want to know what *you,* (he pointed at me) Harold, are doing in my livingroom with my wife."

I was hurt. It was as though my best friend did not trust me.

I told him, "Charlene was devastated when you didn't get home last night. She called me to see if I could do anything to track you down. To see if you were hurt. So, as your best friend, of course I came directly here to comfort and help her."

That was mainly the truth. As you know.

Next Maurice took a bead on Mertz. "And just who, pray tell, is that person over there impersonating an officer?"

Mertz was offended. He flashed his badge at Maurice.

"Lieutenant Mertz, LAPD. And I'm standing here trying to figure out what to charge you with."

Maurice was flabbergasted.

"Charge me with? Like what?"

"Maybe impersonating a corpse. You were supposed to be strangled. And sprawled out on the pavement with a hardon."

Maurice delivered his next lines like the pro he is. And in doing so, wounded my feelings.

"I'm not strangled. I am very much alive. And in my own home. And wondering very much what my so-called friend here was doing comforting my wife."

"Maurice," I objected. "I *am* your best friend. I thought you would want me to comfort Mrs. Delatour since you were murdered."

"Are you mad?" Maurice thundered. "Are you all mad? Do I look like I've been murdered?

Mertz answered honestly. "Unfortunately, no."

Charlene's relief at having her husband safe and sound after her hours of anguish in my arms began to sound a tiny bit tinged with suspicion.

"Tell me, then, Maurice," she asked. "Kindly explain why you have been missing for so long. And what are you doing in that ridiculous attire?"

"Of course I will explain, My Dear," he said, drawing himself up to his full stature (which isn't very high).

"Well?" Charlene replied in what was nearly a challenge.

Maurice hedged.

"In front of all these people?"

Charlene held her ground.

"I think you owe us all an explanation," the little lady demanded. "All three of us have been very concerned about you."

Maurice gave Mertz and me the fisheye, but decided not to say whatever he was thinking.

"Oh, all right," he sighed. "If I must. You see, we were finishing up a scene at the studio yesterday afternoon for Love on the Left Bank."

I shot a look at Charlene and she nodded back that I had informed her right on that score.

"Following take after take, we finally got the flight into the sewers scene right."

Another series of nods between Charlene and me.

"The producer and director had to go to Las Vegas to meet with a syndicate of backers as soon as we wrapped up the shoot. They were going to take the train."

I could see that Charlene was beginning to buy his cockamamie story.

Maurice was on a roll. "I naturally offered to drive them to the Union Station."

"Naturally," Charlene echoed.

I could see that Maurice was pleased that his wife was on his side now.

He really warmed up to his story then, with quiet encouragement from Charlene all the way.

"At the depot, I walked the producer and director out to their boarding ramp. The train wasn't scheduled to leave right away, so they offered to buy me a drink in the club car before leaving. They wanted to thank me for hauling them to the station."

"Of course," Charlene enthused.

In his best thespian voice, Maurice emoted, "And what do you know! To my dismay, the train started going before I could get off."

"Oh, my," Charlene sympathized.

"I couldn't jump off. I would have broken a leg. Or even my neck."

"Poor darling," from Charlene.

"Bullshit," under our breath from Mertz and me.

"As soon as the train got to Vegas, I took the very next one back here to L.A. I didn't call you because I thought I'd be right back."

"How thoughtful," Charlene sighed.

"But *this* train was not an express," Maurice continued. "It stopped at every watering hole in the desert. Barstow, Victorville, Zzyxx."

Mertz and I both blurted out, "Zzyxx?"

Maurice was in his element. "It even stopped at all the ghost towns. Dozens of them," he elaborated.

I could tell Mertz was going nuts with this unlikely story. He threw Maurice what he thought was a curve.

"Oh, yeah? Let's see you explain away those fancy duds you're wearing."

"Oh, these?" Maurice didn't really lose a beat. "That's another story."

"I'll bet it is," Mertz scoffed.

"The return train was full of gamblers," Maurice explained. "All losers. They'd been taken for every cent they had at the tables in Las Vegas."

Charlene was still with him. "Poor baby," she sympathized. "All alone with those awful gamblers."

"Well I didn't trust that crew," the accomplished liar continued. "Not one bit. But I was exhausted. Tired to the bone. And I fell into a deep sleep. And when I awoke, my clothes had been stolen right off my body. There I was. No clothes, no keys, no wallet. The gamblers had all gotten off the train and left me with only these oversized clothes. Which I put on to cover my embarrassing nudity. When the train pulled into the station in L.A., I caught a taxi right here. I didn't want you to worry, Dear."

I could tell Mertz wasn't buying it. Who would? Other than Charlene, of course.

"That's your story?" Mertz asks.

"Of course it's my story. You just heard me tell it, didn't you?"

Mertz was ready for him this time.

"There's just one little point that seems to need clearing up," Mertz said.

Maurice sneered. "'One little point?' I don't think so. My story holds together. Doesn't it Charlene and Horace?"

"Oh, yes," Charlene agreed.

I was anxious to get on his good side, patted him on the back, and said, "Right on, Friend. I believe you."

But I knew Mertz was baiting his hook. And I was secretly rooting for him. You'd never know it, though, from the way I was beaming at Maurice.

"It seems to me that one little point doesn't quite fit," Mertz continued. "You say you were on a train from Vegas. And your clothes were stolen right off your body?"

"That is correct, Officer."

"Then how come they found them on the sidewalk at Eleven Topanga Canyon Boulevard?" the policeman shot at Maurice.

Poor Maurice nearly choked on that one. He even nearly lost his French accent.

"Topanga Canyon...?"

Mertz added, "Boulevard."

Maurice did his best to recover.

"Well, I'll admit. That is a bit difficult to explain."

"Try," the policeman urged.

"Was I in my clothes when they were found there?" Maurice asked.

Mertz had to agree he wasn't.

"Then," Maurice replied with a grand flourish, "How should I know? I wasn't there."

Charlene trotted over to the bundle of clothes that had been left by the trashman.

"Here they are, Dear. Why don't you go put *these* clothes on?"

"I certainly will," Maurice said. "If you will all excuse me, I'll go into the bedroom and change out of these and into these."

Mertz snatched the clothes away.

"Oh no you don't," he growled. "You can't have these."

"Why not?" Maurice said indignantly. "They're mine."

"No they aren't," Mertz declared. "They're evidence."

"What do you mean, evidence? Evidence of what? It's my stolen clothing."

"Stolen, eh?" Mertz exulted. "If they were stolen, that's a theft. And thievery is a crime. So these clothes are evidence of a crime and stay with the LAPD until the case is solved."

"Wait a moment, here," Maurice said. "LAPD? It just occurs to me that you're from the Los Angeles Police Department. We're in Beverly Hills here. You don't have any jurisdiction in this community. We have our own police department. Get out of my house."

I had to agree with my best friend's conclusion. As a matter of fact, I also needed to wheedle my way back into Maurice's good graces again. He apparently hadn't quite bought my story of why I was there with his wife.

So I said to Mertz, "I think Mr. Delatour should have his clothes back, Lieutenant. There are some unanswered questions. But I think my friend does need his clothes. And he may have a point about the jurisdiction in this case."

Mertz was reluctant. But he really knew he didn't have a case. Or any authority in Beverly Hills. And Maurice seemed grateful for my help. I could tell he probably wasn't going to suspect me of fucking his wife. After all, I was his best friend and his 'best boy.'

Mertz took his leave, clearly unhappy that he had no murder case to solve. Poor guy.

Maurice went off to the bedroom to change clothes.

Charlene and I were alone in the livingroom.

"Oh, Horace," she said. "I'm so relieved."

"So am I, Charlene," I said, grabbing a sneaky feel.

All the excitement had given me a huge thirst.

So I suggested to Charlene that we could probably all use a good stiff drink.

She agreed.

There's a wet-bar in their livingroom, and I went to it, got out the Chivas and some soda, and built three Scotch and sodas.

Charlene and I downed our drinks before Maurice got back. It seems he needed a shower before putting on a sporty outfit. He came back into the livingroom looking great.

I refreshed Charlene's drink and mine and we three sat down to celebrate the apparent happy ending to Maurice's woes. I was relieved Maurice and I were still good friends.

We were into a second round, (actually third round for Charlene and me) when the doorbell rang.

"Will you get it, Horace?' Maurice asked.

"Sure," I said, and went to the door.

I opened the door, and Crusher Carney was there. The actor. And he was wearing a raincoat. What I mean to say, it was clear that he was wearing only a raincoat. There was no evidence that there were any clothes whatsoever under that yellow slicker he had on.

"Can I come in?" he asked.

I let him in.

When he accompanied me into the livingroom, I thought Maurice was gonna faint.

Crusher was in a happy mood. Which made me happy. I don't ever want to see a bruiser like that really angry.

When Crusher caught sight of Maurice, he burst into a big smile.

"Oh, hi, Maurice," he said."I was hoping you'd be home."

Maurice indicated that he hadn't met Crusher before. It can happen here in Tinseltown. One actor who happens not to have met another. Rare, but possible.

Maurice was cool as a cucumber.

"How do you do. You must be Mr. Carney, known as Crusher. It's a pleasure."

He got up to greet the Crusher, but thought better than to shake that massive hand.

Crusher answered.

"I've got a question for you Maurice."

Maurice looked both puzzled and anxious.

"A question?"

"Yeah. Why did you make off with my clothes?"

"Clothes?" Maurice bluffed. "What clothes?"

Crusher said, "Those clothes of mine you were wearing when you left that place on Topanga Canyon Boulevard."

Charlene, ever the gracious hostess, said, "Those must be the clothes you had on when you got back from Las Vegas, Dear."

Crusher acknowledged Charlene's presence.

"Hi. I'm Crusher. You must be Mrs. Maurice. You know if my clothes are here?"

I've gotta give her credit. Charlene stood there facing a several hundred pound gorilla who was garbed only in a yellow raincoat. And she behaved as though he was a thoroughly welcome guest dressed in morning attire.

"I believe so, Mr. Carney." She looked over at Maurice.

"Those tentlike clothes you had on when you returned from Las Vegas, Dear. Did you leave them back in the bedroom?"

Maurice nodded yes, but like a condemned man.

"Just a moment, Mr. Carney, Charlene said. "I'll go get them for you."

And off she hustled to fulfill her hostesslike responsibilities.

She returned immediately with the clothes in hand.

Crusher said he recognized them as his.

"Here you are, then," she said cheerily.

"Maisie got real mad at me," Crusher told us all. "She said I had to come get my clothes back."

"How did you get *this* address to get your clothes?" Maurice asked, truly puzzled at how Crusher had appeared in his livingroom and mucked up his story.

Crusher explained.

"When Rob came bursting into the room at Topanga Canyon, it woke me up. And what he said was 'Shut up Maurice'. And when you spoke back with that German accent of yours (I saw Maurice flinch at that, but with self restraint he didn't shout out 'French') that all the comics make such fun of, I knew who you were. Even without my glasses, I could tell you were you. Hell! You're nearly as famous as me (Maurice turned pale). Even buckass naked like you were, I recognized you. So I called Rob to find out where you live. He knew right away. And here I am."

I guess Crusher isn't a very modest guy. Because he took off that yellow slicker right there in front of us all so he could put on the clothes Charlene had brought to him.

What a sight that guy was. Big? Yeah! I think he'd been a wrestler or something before he became an actor. Anyway, he'd kept his athlete's physique. But what had Charlene's full attention was that guy's shlong. I've seen shlongs before. Who hasn't? But that one could win the Nobel Prize for impressiveness.

All three of us just stood there staring as Crusher nonchalantly put on those clothes that had draped Maurice so comically.

When Crusher was through dressing, he smiled with friendly satisfaction.

"Well," he said. "That takes care of that."

He looked at Charlene.

"Thanks for the clothes, Ma'am. Maisie'll be happy with me again. She said I looked too much like a pervert running around wearing only that there raincoat."

Maurice was clearly anxious for Crusher to leave. The big guy'd already shot a hole in that stupid story about the train to Las Vegas. And I imagine if Crusher had hung around much longer he might have spilled more beans about Maurice's adventures that night.

So Maurice said, "That's fine, Crusher. You run right along back to Maisie's. She's probably waiting for you."

"Yeah. Thanks everybody," and Crusher was out of there. I watched out the window as he got into his Maserati, put on a pair of dark glasses, and drove away.

We all needed another drink after that. I fixed another Chivas and soda for Charlene and me. Maurice mixed himself a daiquiri. He's a guy loves his rum.

With our drinks in hand, we sat down like we were before and just kind of stared at each other, nursing our own thoughts about what had just taken place before our eyes.

And damned if the doorbell didn't ring again. I looked out the window to the street. The car out there wasn't a Maserati. It wasn't Crusher returning for some reason. Whoever it belonged to rang the doorbell.

Maurice wanted me to go answer the door.

When I answered it, there was a man and a woman standing there. It took me a few seconds to recognize the guy. It was that dude who'd written and produced that Crusher movie...Showdown at Yellowknife. Rob Roberts. He had a lady with him.

He didn't know me, of course. But everyone in Hollywood knows him. Successful guy.

Very polite, he said, "Is Mr. Delatour home?"

I told him he was and was going to go tell Maurice and Charlene who was there when the guy just barges in, kind of dragging the lady along with him. I just followed along behind them, real curious about what *this* was going to be about.

When Maurice got a gander at the couple, he looked as unhappy as when Crusher had come in. I could tell he wasn't having a very good day.

Maurice set his drink down and stood up, though. Like a good host. Charlene rose too, a perfect hostess.

It was Charlene who spoke.

"Why Mister Roberts. How nice of you to come by." Gracious as she could be.

Crusher's arrival had obviously raised a lot of questions in Charlene's mind. But nothing got in the way of her receiving guests like the refined hostess she always is.

"Nice to see you, Mrs. Delatour," Rob answered, very politely.

"This is my wife, Willa. I don't believe you two have met."

"How do you do, Mrs. Roberts. Delighted. Won't you sit down?" Charlene invited.

Maurice was having a hard time acting out his part as host. But he bowed that Gallic bow of his towards the lady and said, "How do you do," to both of them.

Roberts and his wife sat down. We all followed suit.

"Nice place you've got here, Maurice," Roberts said.

Maurice didn't answer. But Charlene did, of course.

"How nice of you to say so. Actually we're quite comfortable here. Do you and Mrs. Roberts live here in Beverly Hills?"

"No, we don't, Mrs. Delatour," Rob answered. "My wife Willa and I live in Hollywood."

"You two must call me Charlene," the charming hostess said. "I find that informality goes best with the Southern California lifestyle. Don't you?"

"Yes, I do, Charlene," Rob replied. "And please call me Rob. And my wife Willa favors an informal lifestyle as well, don't you Dear?"

If I've ever seen two uncomfortable people, Mrs. Roberts – Willa

– and Maurice were it. I kept completely out of the discussion. I was enjoying the discomfort of my best friend and of Rob Roberts' wife. Mr. Roberts – Rob – and Charlene seemed perfectly at ease.

"May I offer you anything to drink?" Charlene asked. "I can brew some coffee or tea in a minute. Or, even though it's rather early in the morning, the three of us were enjoying cocktails when you arrived. So, if you'd prefer...?"

"I don't think so, Charlene," Rob said amiably. "How about you, my dear? Would you like some coffee? You apparently had a rather rough night."

Willa just hung her head and wagged it "No."

"Perhaps a bit of rum, Love?" he went on. "I noticed an empty bottle of Bacardi back at that apartment in Topanga Canyon Boulevard. I'll bet you have some Bacardi over there by your wet bar, don't you, Maurice?"

Oh, boy! Was I ever having fun. I'd been trying to piece together the things that I'd seen coming down bit by bit that morning. Maurice out all night. Topanga Canyon. Crusher. Willa. Rum. What a mix. I'm not sure I'll ever be able to straighten it all out. But it was damned entertaining.

The squirm factor between Maurice and Willa could have been registered on the Richter Scale.

Charlene asked the obvious question.

"What is all this about Topanga Canyon...Rob?"

"Oh," Rob replied, nonchalantly. "Didn't Maurice tell you? I'm sorry if I've let a little kitty out of the bag. Well, I guess you're entitled to know. Don't you think so Willa? I'm sure Maurice doesn't want to keep any secrets from his wife. Do you Maurice?"

The silence that hung over the room was delicious. I was absolutely delighted.

Rob held the silence for exactly the right length of time. He's a master showman you know. His movies always top the charts. The critics hate 'em. The public loves 'em.

"You see, Charlene," Rob continued finally. "It seems that my wife and your husband are lovers. Maurice here has a little love shack he keeps over in Topanga Canyon."

Charlene gasped. "Topanga Canyon." Both she and I were beginning to get the drift of things.

Rob continued right on.

"The two lovebirds are apparently head over heels in love. They decided to spend the whole night in each other's arms. Making love and drinking Bacardi. It's a touching love story, don't you think?"

"Oh, my," Charlene exclaimed. She turned pale, but maintained her composure. Willa and Rob looked like they would gladly sink right down into the Oriental rug on the floor. Rob kept his cool, telling his story like a good raconteur.

"Apparently Topanga Canyon was too far way to travel for our enraptured lovers to hold their trysts. Did Maurice happen to tell you he rented an apartment in our building from me just yesterday?"

Charlene shook her head.

"Oh, yes," Rob elaborated. "Exactly downstairs from the apartment where my loving wife and I live.They were making mad love right under the nose, so to speak, of the cuckolded husband. I can see where that would add spice to the liaison. Is that the right word, Maurice? Liaison? Do I pronounce it correctly?"

Rob got no answer to that. Maurice looked like he might have to throw up.

Gee! I don't know when I've had so much fun. That is, other than in bed, of course.

"I've been such a fool," Charlene said.

Maurice came suddenly back to life.

"Ma chérie," he pleaded. "It's not what you think. I love you."

Charlene's voice was soft and modulated. And deadly.

"Don't you 'Ma chérie' me. You...sneak thief. You...phony Frenchman. Not only cheating. But with another man's wife!"

"I understand your dismay, Charlene," Rob soothed. "I believe I share your disgust. But I've had time to think the matter over. And I believe we should deal with the situation rationally. I've mulled it all over and I now realize why Willa and Maurice have done this thing."

Maurice and Willa looked very surprised.

Together and in harmony, they said, "You do?"

I nearly chimed in with "You do?" too. I was interested in how this was all turning out. But I kept my peace. Hell! I hadn't even been acknowledged as being there since I'd let the Roberts in.

Rob went on to explain to everyone why Maurice and Willa had done the down and dirty somewhere off there in Topanga Canyon.

"The two of you," Rob explained to Maurice and Willa, "must be very much in love. Since you are both married, you are star-crossed lovers. Like Romeo and Juliet."

I was really amused by *that* one.

"So," Rob continued. "I believe in being magnanimous. I am going to solve your problem for you."

Here came another pregnant pause. More dramatic than even the last one. Damn! That guy was good. No wonder he's wowing them at the box office.

No one asked how he was going to solve the problem. We all just waited.

"I am not going to stand in the way of these two lovers," Rob declared. "They clearly really deserve each other."

Ouch! That hurt. It stung so good. He really hit home with the couple who were at the center of the drama he was composing. What an *auteur*.

"Therefore, Maurice, I am going to free Willa so you can marry her." Rob offered.

Willa started to protest, but Rob cut her off.

"I've contacted my attorney," Rob told her. "I'm filing for divorce."

Maurice finally had something to say.

"I can't marry her," he protested. "I'm already married."

Charlene put quiet to that line.

"Not for long, you're not," she said icily.

Then to Rob Charlene asked, "Would your lawyer be willing to take another case? I agree that those two deserve each other."

"I'll give you his number," Rob replied. "I'm sure he'll be helpful."

Then, to Maurice, Rob said, "So you see, Maurice. You wanted my wife. Now you can have her!"

Maurice, in his Gallic, chivalrous way, answered, "I can *have* her? I don't even want the bitch."

That was my boy.

Willa began to cry. I would have chuckled out loud, but knew it would not go over well.

Charlene, the dear, went up to Rob and kissed him on the cheek.

"It seems that we have much in common... Rob," she said so sweetly it could melt your heart.

Rob, surprisingly, put his arm around Charlene's waist.

It looked to me like the beginning of a beautiful friendship. One that I hoped would not rob me of future pleasure with one of the better lays in my book.

CHAPTER EIGHT
WILLA ON CAMERA:

Here I am, back in Apartment 123. Right where the ride on this Hollywood merry-go-round began. This room you see is where, in a sense, it all began and ended.

I was no longer married to Rob. My fling with Maurice caused a rupture in my marriage. Rob had what I would call spyware in our apartment upstairs and overheard some remarks Maurice and I had made to each other. He took them out of context, and divorced me.

And if that sounds like a person in denial about the way she messed up – that's what it is. Truth to tell, I had a good marriage and foolishly wrecked it.

Maurice's wife learned of that meeting her husband and I had out in the Valley, and she divorced him.

So Maurice and I were free to marry.

Result: Two wrecked marriages.

Maurice and I are now husband and wife.

Unlike my first husband, Rob Roberts, Maurice does not trust me. At all. He constantly accuses me of being unfaithful. Hah! Talk about the pot calling the kettle greasy. Maurice can't stay faithful when he's out of my sight any more than our presidents can remain faithful to their wives. Men! They're such pigs.

On the day that brought my tale full circle, I was in this very room with my lover, Tex McCall, the famous cowboy actor. I believe I mentioned him to you in a previous screening that Tex McCall of Plano, Texas, is a phony cowboy. He was born Irving Nussbaum of Brooklyn, New York and never rode a horse until he came out here to Hollywood at age eighteen and took lessons. He studied at the Van Nuys Academy of Equitation. That's a horse riding school out in the Valley. He took acting lessons over in Pasadena. He got a dialect coach who converted his Brooklyn accent to plain ol' Texas.

The only thing no one had to teach Irving was to look Texan. He's tall. Six foot four. He's rangy. He has a long, narrow face with high cheekbones. And he'd watched old Gary Cooper, John Wayne, Roy Rogers, and Hopalong Cassidy movies on TV from the time he could toddle. He developed "the walk" from imitating his TV heroes.

I was waiting for him here in Apartment 123 on an April morning. The place was available for rent. Maurice had signed a lease for it back before we were married, you know. But he didn't need it any more, because, well, because as my husband he now manages The Emperor's Arms.

I'd waited for my Texas loverboy in this room that morning for nearly fifteen minutes. It was part of our fantasy that he came to me from off the range, and was often delayed by a stampede over on Sunset Boulevard or a fight with Indians in the Hollywood Bowl.

I caught the sound of his boots clanging down the outside corridor.

He had just narrowly escaped from a run-in with a gang of desperados over on Sepulveda Boulevard and found his way back to the One-Two-Three Ranch. I opened the door and welcomed him into my waiting arms.

"Are you all right, Tex?" I asked breathless.

"Just wounded, O my darling," he drawled. "Big Dick McGoon's gang ambushed me down Sepulveda Way. I managed to get a dozen of 'em. But Big Dick is still out there. We agreed to meet at the Crenshaw Corral at high noon. In the meantime, I needed to come see my darlin' in what may be our last embrace."

In Tex's last movie, Showdown in Loredo, Tex played the role he always plays. Tex McCall, the rangy cowboy from Plano. Crusher Carney played Big Dick McGoon, the toughest cattle rustler east of the Pecos "One last kiss before I go to my shootout with Big Dick," my Texan hero requested.

He took me in his arms and pressed his lips to mine. As our tongues met, he deepened the kiss by pressing his manly Western tongue hard against mine.

We pulled apart and flung our clothes off our bodies in our desperate need to unite in love for what might be our last embrace before the shootout at the Crenshaw Corral.

My lover stood facing me. In all his gorgeous maleness. Not an ounce of fat on him. Muscles sculpted like Apollo. His abs a perfect sixpack. His pects, delts, biceps... God! He talks about those muscles all the time. You'd think I could remember their names. But it's all like Greek.

I can't remember what all those damned muscles are called. But I sure know how to feel them. I knew he hadn't earned a single one of those gorgeous muscles rounding up dogies on the range. He paid handsomely for them at Brewster's Gym up on Vine and made a rich man of his personal trainer, Rip Hanks, who sculpted him like a great artist.

But I couldn't argue with the result. Even though I knew each muscle was in that shape because it was bought and paid for with Hollywood dollars.

Visually Tex is a doll. My God! That man is a sight to behold. We stood there in the livingroom, naked as lovebirds, me absorbed by that luscious torso of his. He was concentrating on flexing his muscles.

Just as before we got together after my divorce from Rob, Tex springs that long, robust cowboy hardon every time he walks into the room and sees me.

I ran my fingers over those perfect cheekbones of his. He flexed his biceps. I nibbled on his manly earlobe. I think it may have been his triceps or something he flexed. I ran my tongue across his perfectly sculpted pectoral muscles, with the obligatory encircling and nibbling on his nipples.

As always, I take that handsome dong in my hands and give him a few gentle strokes. He picks me up, then, in his strong, manly hands and hauls me over to the bed. He sets me back down on the floor, lies down on the bed and I mount that prick like he was the saddle and I take his saddlehorn into my cunt.

"Hey, there, Pardner," I said. "Know where I can find any Cayuse around here?"

I wasn't really sure what a "Cayuse" was. And I doubt Tex knew, or cared, either. In Hollywood not much has to be really real anyway.

I suggested that the cayuse might be found in the rodeo.

So, we had what we called our "rodeo."

As our rodeo wound down, Tex had a question for me.

"Say, Gal. Is this here apartment for rent by any chance?"

"Yep!"

"Why don't I rent it so we'll have it for our love corral 'stead of havin' to always mosey down to my place in Tarzana."

"You'll have to see my husband, Maurice, about that," I told him. "Come up to our place at 223 this afternoon. Maurice will take care of the details."

That afternoon Tex visited Maurice and me. Maurice rented the place to him, aware of just what was going on.

And that completed a full turn of the merry-go-round. This time I guess Tex got the brass ring.

But I know that the carrousel never remains stuck in one place for long. It will continue to circle around and around as long as there's a Tinsel Town. And as for myself? I plan to ride it...and ride it...and ride it...

PART THREE

QUEEN OF THE DANCE

CHAPTER ONE

Doctor Ralph Harlow was not a happy man. He was relatively comfortable financially. He lived in a home in Hollywood on Franklin Avenue that, while not a mansion, was certainly more upscale than anything he had ever imagined for himself. He had a thriving chiropractic practice there in Hollywood. One would think he'd be happy.

But Ralph could not be happy when he was feeling horny. It was Thursday, and he craved action. And he knew he would be getting no loving from his wife Emma that day. She had "done her duty" the previous day. Wednesday was her day. "Never on Thursday."

Back before he was married, Ralph Harlow had a fairly active sex life. In high school, he and his best friend Eddie Gomez pursued sex with a passion. They even had a rivalry with each other to see who could score the most sex points with the girls.

Most males lie about their sex lives. But not Ralph and Eddie. Each reported faithfully and truly, and kept up a fierce competition with each other all the way through school.

To score points, Ralph concentrated on the chubby chicks in school.

They didn't get much action from the jocks or the Big Men on Campus (the BMOCs), so could occasionally agree to be romanced by the likes of Ralph. Eddie concentrated on the girls who lacked social skills or were shy. He did pretty well fishing in that sea.

In fairness to the girls, it must be said the two boys did no harm. The girls they entertained were never forced. They were compliant and welcomed the attention. And they forever after felt a warm spot in their hearts for the swains who had so ardently petted, groped, felt up, and fucked them.

Eddie got the most poontang. Ralph managed to get blown about half the times, scored a fuck about a quarter of the times, and batted out the rest of the times back in high school. When he graduated and started working, his screwing average just about doubled.

Ralph met Emma after he graduated from high school. He had a job bagging groceries at a supermarket. One of the checkers at the market, Patty, had known Emma at school and greeted her friendlily whenever she came through the line.

Ralph and Patty sometimes had coffee together at a Starbucks close to the store. He'd gotten into Patty's pants a half-dozen time. One time, when they were lying in bed after he'd come once and brought her to orgasm twice, Patty, in making conversation, told him that Emma's parents had been tragically killed in a plane crash, leaving her very well off.

Ralph was on a road to nowhere in his job. He thought about Emma. She fit into both his own and Eddie's categories. She was somewhat obese and rather socially awkward. But apparently had lots of dough.

One thing led to another. Ralph got Patty to introduce him to Emma. Emma was not getting any dates, and agreed to go out with Ralph.

With this gal, though, Eddie's game was not seduction. He decided that very early in their dating. And Emma had made it quite clear – no marriage, no sex. Not even a decent feel. Blow job? Are you kidding. Something that Emma could never bring herself to do. No matter how few dates she was getting. (Like none.)

Oh, well. A guy has to feather his nest as best he can.

Emma had a need of her own. She felt a need for a husband. One she could control. And she knew right away she could keep this grocery bagger under her thumb. So she decided she would marry Ralph. And she did.

Ralph discovered that Emma had many fine points. She had a sweet way of talking that disguised her rigid need to control. She was quite spiritual and concerned about such matters as world peace and the spiritual transformation of the masses. These did not happen to be subjects that interested Ralph one whit. But they were, he happened to agree, fine points. Although not something to give a guy a hardon.

Emma's relative financial flushness did matter to Ralph a great deal. He had always been a bit cash-challenged and craved a better life than the one available to a grocery bagger.

In their discussions, Emma let it be known that when they got married, she would pay for him to attend chiropractic college. She herself was a firm advocate of chiropractic, which relieved her chronic back problem. Upon graduation from that college, she would set him up in a practice. She thought Hollywood would be an ideal place for such a practice. She understood, correctly, that the studio workers there, the gaffers, dolly grips, carpenters, and others in the trades were subject to straining their backs.

And, best of all, Madame Zlatsky had her ashram in Hollywood. And Emma seldom missed a séance at Madame Zlatsky's.

Ralph agreed to everything. He would marry her. He would go to chiropractic college. Emma would keep control of all the money. Everything they had would be in her name. Emma would control the finances, Ralph's time. Everything.

Ralph got two concessions from Emma. They would have sex on Wednesdays and he would have freedom to go to his lodge meetings twice a month.

Emma had asked Madame Zlatsky's advice about those two conditions.

"Sexual activity does deplete your aura," she was told. "But once a week, if you don't get aroused yourself, you won't harm the orange of your aura too much," the Madame advised her. "And a husband has a right to his nasty need once a week. And men, pigs that they are, need male bonding to keep healthy. Let this Ralph person go to his stupid lodge meetings a couple of times a month."

So, although Doctor Ralph Harlow was not a happy man, he had bought into his situation and strove to live with his incessant horniness as best he could. And, he was looking forward to the first Friday of the month with drooling anticipation.

Now *there* was something to make him happy.

On the first Friday of every month, he and Eddie went to their lodge meeting. They were members of the Secret, Benevolent, Loyal Order of the

Muskrat (SBLOM). As a matter of fact, they were the only members of that organization since they had invented it themselves as a ruse for Ralph to get out from under Emma's thumb a couple of times a month and strive to get laid.

Eddie had not married, having been blessed with better financial resources than his friend and lodge brother, he had never felt the need. So he had freedom that Ralph could not help but covet.

On Friday evening, Ralph could hardly wait for six o'clock. At six promptly, Eddie came by the Franklin Avenue home to pick up his best buddy to head off for the mystic rites of their lodge meeting.

Lodge meetings were held at different venues at different times. But always in the City of Caborca Gardens.

Caborca Gardens is a small city occupying somewhat less than three square miles of earth. It takes about an hour and a half to drive there from Hollywood. The San Bernardino Freeway, Interstate Highway Ten, shoots East from Los Angeles, affording easy access to the small city.

Caborca Gardens is supported by one industry. Female flesh. It is crammed with topless bars and lapdance clubs. The liberal view of the town's local government is much more lenient about the display of female nudity than any other community in Southern California. And it is located in San Bernardino County, which has always been much less stuffy about such things than neighboring Los Angeles County. Indeed, until World War Two put a stop to it, San Bernardino was the only county in Southern California with legal whore houses.

On their drive to Caborca Gardens, the opening topic of discussion for the two friends was invariably initiated by the question, "Are you getting any lately?"

Eddie regaled his friend with tales of the tail he had been chasing since the last time they were together. He was happy to give Ralph the details on special techniques his dates were proficient in, such as the arts of imaginative fucking, cock sucking, anal sex, mutual masturbation, and muff diving availability. Ralph had little to add from his own sparse experiences.

Eddie was a podiatrist. His family had been affluent enough to send him to podiatry college. And, on graduation, he, like his buddy Ralph, chose Hollywood as the venue for his practice. He correctly reasoned that dancers and starlets would require a professional to help them maintain beautiful feet. And, of course, the community has always had its share of denizens with fallen arches, ingrown toenails, and the other ills that befall feet in our times.

Eddie had at least his share of willing young ladies traipsing into his clinic to avail themselves of his expertise. And, after working hours, he frequented the bars and clubs that abound in the Hollywood area. And more often than not he "got lucky" during his bar hops.

Thus his juicy tales of romance could usually fill the hour and a half drive to Caborca Gardens.

Ralph was not silent on the drive. He commented on his friend's adventures. And filled the air with his own woes.

Eddie would say something like, "And how about you. Getting any at all?"

Ralph told about the little bit he was getting on the side. Sometimes a patient. Occasionally one of the girls who worked at the clinic. But the little romances were always furtive. There was more groping than screwing. Always with the threat of Emma's inquisitive eye discovering his mini-flings. His sex life was scarcely enough to keep a man robust and healthy. Most of the time it was only the uninspired Wednesday matinée with his wife that gave him any satisfaction at all.

So Caborca Gardens provided a Garden of Eden in Ralph's otherwise bleak sexual landscape.

Ralph's financial comfort was absolutely dependent on keeping Emma from leaving him. And he was sure she would pack up her moneybags and walk out if he was ever discovered "wandering."

But he cherished one hope. He had a very rich uncle, Unkie Al Pughworthy, a millionaire relative dwelling in Madrazo, Arizona. Unkie Al had made a tremendous fortune from the open-pit copper mine he owned in Madrazo. Unkie Al had never shown great fondness for Ralph. But Ralph kept a flicker of hope alive that his rich uncle would make him his heir.

Of the many palaces of entertainment in Caborca, the Hollywood friends had settled on the Pussywillow Club as their favorite.

As they parked in the lot next to the club, Ralph told his buddy his plans for the evening.

And on this particular trip, he planned to really have himself a time.

"Look, Eddie," Ralph said. "This time here, I'm going the whole way."

"You mean the Priapus Room?"

"Yep. So I'll arrange for the van to take me home after the club closes. Don't wait for me."

"Good luck, Pal. And enjoy the ride," was all the answer he got.

Eddie knew all about the Priapus Room, but had never felt it worth his while to shell out the kind of dough needed to enter that very private place.

When they entered the club, Ralph made arrangements with the bouncer for a ride home in the van at the end of what he hoped would be a very festive evening. The club provided two way transportation service from the club to Los Angeles and Hollywood. The cost was nominal. Getting customers to Caborca Gardens from the megalopolis was essential for business.

The Muskrats found that their favorite table was available and sat down.

For the price of a fifty dollar bottle, each, of local vintage "champagne," a totally nude dancer would visit their table. She would jiggle, boogie, shake, and flounce in close proximity.

Gentlemen clients are aware that in order to get more than an eyeful, they need to come bearing a walletfull of fifty dollar bills.

Ralph always came loaded. Although Emma kept tight watch on the books at the office, Ralph had figured out over a dozen ways to skim money from the till undetected. He set up a secret, private account at a bank and had amassed several thousand dollars in it. And he had a debit card attached to the account for "emergencies." His life with Emma would scarcely have been worth living without access to the cash that funded his lodge activities.

The boys' favorite dancer was Kinkie Lamour. She had a pixie face framed with mischief. She was five foot one, ninety-eight pounds, with perky breasts, a gorgeous ass, and legs to die for. She was, in the words of the Muskrats, "Awesome." Her eyes were green in color and her hair a strawberry blonde stubble. She kept her hair cut to what is known as a Number One Buzz. It was the same cut Ralph had worn since he was a teen-ager. He always got a head rub from Kinkie when she came to his table in celebration of their identical haircuts.

It wasn't long before Kinkie came to the boys' table. Her only attire was a small gold handbag which she carried with a flair. The sight of her perfect nude figure always elicited a happy response from the Muskrats' groins.

Ralph and Eddie knew the rules. The dancers could touch the customers but, within the confines of the auditorium, the customers could not touch the girls. The vigilant bouncers enforced the rules, politely but firmly. The town fathers of Caborca Gardens were not going to allow public fondling. The breaking of the decency laws of the State of California could jeopardize the main economy of their community.

Kinkie approached Eddie with a smile. As a regular, she had learned from him his name and occupation.

"Eddie-boy. You're looking mighty good tonight."

"You do too, Kinkie."

"Yeah," she answered. "Every time I see you here, I get so hot."

Kinkie set her handbag on the table.

Eddie knew Kinkie was only feeding him a line. But he loved playing the game. He took a fifty dollar bill from his wallet and slipped it into the purse's opening.

"Oh, Eddie," she responded. "You certainly *do* know all the moves. What would you like?"

Both the boys wanted the same thing. Kinkie knew what it was but always asked anyway.

"How 'bout the Bootie Song?" Eddie asked.

"Sure, Big Boy," she said. The DJ was very aware of what dancers were doing what where. When Kinkie flipped a hip in his direction he deftly shifted the music into the Bootie Song.

Kinkie favored Eddie by singing the song directly to him, maintaining a provocative pose that seemed unique to her.

"Shake your bootie to the North. *(bump)*
Shake your bootie to the South. *(bump)*
Shake your bootie to the East and West.*(grind)*
Well shut my mouth."

On the word "mouth," Kinkie's hand went to her mouth, she faced away from Eddie, and gently lowered that beautifully rounded behind of hers to within a centimeter or so of his lap. Her dance then went on as she fluttered her nude bottom over his crotch area. The boys' peckers rose beyond the centimeter distance until Kinkie's cunt was rubbing over their boners in a most delightful way. The dance lasted five minutes.

With eighteen-year-olds who managed to scrape up enough money to enjoy the attractions of the Pussywillow Club, the lapdance often lasted about a minute. At that age, it is seldom possible to withstand much more than sixty seconds with a luscious female dancing in your lap. A splotch of cum on the trousers was a sure thing.

Both the Muskrats were mature enough to soldier through a five minute performance. Eddie enjoyed his five minutes worth to the end. Ralph had come

133

during the dance a few times. Exquisite.

The conclusion of the dance was signaled by Kinkie facing him and lowering those perky breasts to an inch or so from his mouth as she sang, "Shut my mouth."

Eddie's tongue was too slow to get a lick at those inviting mounds. The bouncers were always willing to overlook a rapid tongue-flick. But you had to be quick about it.

It was Ralph then who slipped a fifty dollar bill into the gaping mouth of the handbag.

The song and dance he received was close to identical to the one his lodge brother had enjoyed. Except that he managed to get the dessert of a tongue-flick over a rosy nipple before Kinkie pulled away. And his peckerhead was moist with pre-come.

The boys usually stayed at the club for about two hours. That was as long as the champagne and their stamina lasted. But on this particular occasion, Ralph started ordering straight shots of brandy to accompany his bubbly. He was ready to really party.

Kinkie managed to get to their table about every twenty minutes. The bottle of local "champagne," five or six lapdances, and in Ralph's case five shots of brandy, and it was time for the party to come to an end.

When Eddie had consumed his bubbly, he excused himself to go to the restroom to jack off.

When Eddie returned to the table, relieved and cleansed, Ralph was finishing the champagne in his bottle and his fifth brandy. He assured his buddy that he was all right and in high anticipation of the experience awaiting him in the Priapus Room with Kinkie. Eddie said he would check in on him at his home the next morning and departed the club.

Ralph used his debit card to pay for the private session he would have with his favorite dancer in the room with the locked door. He parted with five hundred dollars for the privilege.

The civic authorities of Caborca Gardens have no curiosity about what goes on between consenting adults behind closed doors. San Bernardino County has never completely relinquished its past.

Ralph knew pretty well what went on behind that closed door. But because he had ingested way too much alcohol before entering, he never did remember what happened to him in there. He had to rely on what Kinkie later told him happened. And he never knew how much to believe of her tales about the wild time they had that evening and into the early hours of the next day.

CHAPTER TWO

The next thing Ralph did remember was an awareness of waking up on the couch in his own livingroom with his friend Eddie shaking him. He was fully clothed. But the clothes were badly rumpled.

"Come on, Buddy. Wake up!" Eddie was urging. "It's getting a bit late in the morning and you have a new day to face."

Ralph's view of his friend was sadly out of focus. The pain in his head was severe. His mouth was dry. And his stomach was very sour.

"Go away, Eddie," he groaned. "Just leave me here to die."

"You're not going to die, Pal," Eddie assured him. "You'll just wish you could for a while. You'll get over it."

Ralph was just enough with it to wonder how Eddie got into his house.

"Easy," Eddie told him. "I rang your doorbell. No one answered. I tried the door, it was unlocked. I came in, saw the condition you were in and went into that bathroom over there to look for some aspirin or Alka-Seltzer for you. Here, take these pills I found and wash 'em down with this."

Eddie had brought a very welcome glass of water to the coffee table next to the couch along with a couple of aspirin.

Neither man noticed that there was a dress draped over the back of the couch. They would become aware of it in due time.

Ralph sat up, holding his head with both hands. He managed to get the two pills down and welcomed the effect the water had on his dry mouth. The aspirin was fine, but he felt a need for an Alka-Seltzer to settle his stomach.

The throbbing in his head was intense, but he was beginning to believe his friend that he would survive. And at that moment the front door opened and in breezed Ralph's wife Emma in her customary overly-cheery mood.

"Oh, Ralphsie," Emma chirped. "I see you're up and dressed finally. My but you *did* sleep in, didn't you? Hello, Eddie. How are you?"

Ralph groaned and Eddie acknowledged that he was just fine, thank you.

Emma continued in her annoyingly cheerful tone.

"Ralph, Honey. You *do* look a mess, don't you? Why in the world did you put on such rumpled clothes this morning? And you didn't even bother to shave."

Emma took Ralph's face with a hand on each cheek and brought him close for a peck of a kiss. The act caused an intense pain to rise from Ralph's neck to the top of his head. But he stifled his groan.

When Emma caught a whiff of his breath she changed her mind about the kiss.

"My, my," she grimaced. "Don't we smell awful this morning? And that green tinge to your skin. Not a very becoming shade for you, Dear. He does look ghastly, doesn't he Eddie?"

"Just a bit of a sour stomach, Emma," Ralph extemporized. "They served a pepperoni pizza at the lodge hall last night and it didn't seem to agree with me. Do we have any pepto or alka in the house? I could use something to settle my stomach."

Emma expressed some surprise.

"I got up early this morning to go to Madame Zlatsky's," Emma chirped on. "The Madame held a séance at nine o'clock. Afterward I went shopping on Rodeo Drive. Chez Cerise is having a sale and I didn't want to miss any bargains. Anyway, before I left the house before going out to the Madame's and Chez Cerise, I just had to stop by your bedroom and give a kissy-kiss to my Ralphie Ralph. Hims was all snuggled down in his covers. Emma gave her sweets a nice little good morning kiss on the top of hims head. I never would have guessed you weren't feeling well then."

That made Ralph wonder.

"You came into my bedroom and kissed me?" he asked, a bit

bewildered.

Emma was cold as an eel sexually. She was domineering and totally manipulative.But she was full of sharp little kisses and lovey-dovey expressions. She called everyone from shop girls to bank presidents "Dear," or "Honey," or "Love." Ralph was surprised to hear that she had kissed him in the bedroom that morning. He had assumed that he had fallen asleep on the couch when he staggered home from the binge in Caborca Gardens in his drunken condition. He pointed to the bedroom door.

"You kissed me in there?" he asked. "And I didn't wake up?"

"No, no, you silly-willy. You didn't wake up at all. You were all rolled up in a bunch of blankets. All I could see was the top of your cute little head. So I just brushed a kiss on your head and bustled out. And I come back to find my Ralphie with a tummy ache. Poor Dear. Well, I'll just go get an antacid of some kind for you in my bathroom. First we'll get that tum-tum all well again. Then you can go get into some clothes that are more presentable. No, first let's brush those toofies and shave. Did you shower this morning? You don't smell like it. Well, first let's get you well again..."

Still talking as she was leaving the room, Emma traipsed off to do her Florence Nightingale bit for her distressed husband.

Ralph and Eddie did not have to wait long to discover a clue about why Emma thought she had kissed her husband in the bedroom when they assumed he had been on the couch in the livingroom all morning. Because Kinkie happened to be in the bedroom and had been awakened by all the chatter in the next room.

Kinkie sat up in bed, stretched, and did nothing to suppress a hearty yawn.

"What the Hell?" the Muskrats exclaimed in unison.

Ralph roused himself from his couch and led the way to the bedroom door. He quietly opened the door and the two Muskrats peeked in.

Kinkie was immediately aware of them and favored them with her most dazzling smile.

"Well, Boys. You two *are* a sight to wake up to."

She got out of bed, completely nude.

Eddie was amused. Ralph was flabbergasted.

"You are looking wonderful, Miss Kinkie," Eddie said.

In censorious tones Ralph said, "My God! What are *you* doing there?"

Kinkie looked coy. "Ralph! What a way to talk. After what we've been to each other."

Eddie intervened.

"I'm afraid my friend here is a bit out of sorts. I'm sure he doesn't mean to be rude. But apparently he does not recall that you accompanied him home last night."

"Good morning, Eddie," Kinkie smiled. *"You're* nice.Not like old Mister Grouch there. When you left me in his care last night, he literally lifted me in his arms and carried me to the Priapus Room. It was terrific. Like Superman and Lois Lane. Your friend's really strong. Did you know that? You wouldn't think so looking at him the way he's kind of scrawny and all.

"And once he got me in that room, he really *was* Superman. Jesus! What a lover! I've never known such a virile lover...We were no sooner in the room than he was sucking my tits. You suck real nice, did you know that Ralphie. So, to reward you, I got down on my knees and sucked your..."

Ralph cut her off.

"See here, You. There's no need to be coarse. After all, you're here in my home. And I don't know how you even got here."

"'Coarse' am I?" Kinkie answered with mock disdain. "It wasn't *my* idea to come here. When Lance -- he's the club owner you know. When Lance came to that room we were in to tell you it was time to get your butt to the van, you wiped off your cock, got your clothes back on and went into your Superman or Batman act or whatever and carried me bodily to the van. You wouldn't let me get out. And in the van, even though there were six other guys in there, you were all over me all the way from Caborca Gardens to here. You promised you wouldn't calm down until I gave you a blowjob. When we got here, you passed out on the couch and I just curled up here in the bed and had myself a nice snooze."

Neither of the Muskrats believed a word of what Kinkie was saying. Ralph had been soused, all right. But probably even sober he wouldn't have been as vigorously physical or sexual as the young lady claimed. Or would he?

Ralph was appalled. Eddie was highly amused.

To her credit, the truth was that Kinkie thought Ralph was kind of cute. And she was genuinely concerned about his condition. So she accompanied him in the van to make sure he got home all right. But she would never admit to such a soft streak in herself.

She went on. "Then, pretty early this morning, you just couldn't get enough loving. You sneaked into the bedroom and kissed me on top of the head. What an old darling you are."

"Christ Almighty!" Ralph exclaimed. "That wasn't me that kissed you. That was my wife."

"What a sweetie she must be, then," Kinkie said. "Most wives wouldn't be that understanding. I can hardly wait to meet her."

"That would be the worst disaster I could ever face," Ralph said. "Emma must not know you are here or were ever here."

At that point, all three heard Emma's voice in the distance. She was saying, "Are you decent, Dear? I'm coming in with something to soothe that nasty feeling old tum-tum."

Ralph was truly alarmed. The Apocalypse seemingly was at hand.

"Damn, damn, damn" he said. "My wife's coming in here. Look, you have to hide. You can't be found here. Particularly in that lewd, nude state you're in. Go away somewhere."

"Oh, the nice lady who kissed me on the head this morning?" Kinkie enthused. "I'd love to meet her."

"You just stay right there in bed," Ralph said. "Come on, Eddie. Let's get back into the livingroom and keep Emma from coming in here and discovering *that*!"

"Well, I certainly don't like being called 'that' after all those sweet intimacies we shared," Kinkie said in mock indignation.

Kinkie hadn't finished her sentence when Ralph and Eddie were out the door. Ralph got the door closed and had scooted back to the sofa when Emma walked in with a tray. On the tray were a glass of water and a bottle of Pepto-Bismol.

"Here we go, Dear," Emma warbled.

When she got a look at him, she was mock distressed. "Oh, Ralphsie. Still in those rumpled old clothes. Tsk, tsk. Hims gots a tummy ache. Here! Mamma make hims feel all well again."

Ralph was grateful for the Pepto, and got it down. Now, his task was to get Emma out of the house so he could smuggle the lapdancer out of there.

"There," he said. "That's better. I might as well get showered and shaved now.So why don't you go back to Madame Zlatsky's. Or to Chez Cerise? Yes, that's a good idea. Go back and buy yourself something nice."

Emma was not inclined to leave.

"Where I'm going is out to the kitchen to fix myself a bite to eat. Would either of you like me to bring you a sandwich?"

The boys declined the offer.

Emma was about to leave when she saw Kinkie's dress folded on the sofa.

"What is *that* doing there?" Emma asked.

Ralph noticed the dress for the first time, and guessed immediately what it was. He just looked at it in horror, and could not come out with a reasonable answer.

"Oh, Ralphsie," Emma chirped on. "Here hims feeling all tummy ached. And Chez Cerise sent my dress here and he had to get up and sign for it. Louise at Chez Cerise told me it was coming, but I didn't think it would get here so soon."

Ralph was relieved at the apparent solution to the question of the dress. But was horrified when Emma grabbed the dress and walked away with it.

"Where are you going with that?" he asked.

Emma held the tiny dress up next to her large frame.

"Tsk, tsk! That Louise," she complained. "This is the wrong dress. I could never get into it. I'm going to take it back next time I'm at Rodeo Drive."

And with that, the dress was whisked out of the room.

And as soon as Emma was gone with the dress, Kinkie came bouncing into the room.

Despite his throbbing head, Ralph was able to think. And he knew what needed to be done.

"You've got to get out of here. Now! Before my wife gets back."

"I know when I'm not wanted," Kinkie spit back. "I can see what kind of man you are. Use a girl, fuck her like a madman, and then toss her away like rubbish. All right, Mister Meanie. I'm outta here."

Eddie had to stand up for his friend.

"I hope you don't take my friend wrong, Miss Kinkie. He's not feeling well. And he's concerned about saving his marriage. If Mrs. Harlow weren't here, we'd both be delighted for you to stay indefinitely."

"You're so nice, Eddie," she answered. "*You* know how to treat a lady. Next time you're at the club, I'll see that you get very special treatment. Just see if I don't. Now I'll just get dressed and get out of here. In the meantime, why doesn't one of you call a taxi for me? And it seems to me the least you could do is pay my taxi fare home."

"Quite right," Eddie agreed.

"Now, where's my dress?" Kinkie asked.

"Oh Hell!" Ralph cried.

"What do you mean, 'Oh Hell'?" Kinkie asked.

"Your dress," Ralph lamented. "My wife took it with her."

Emma was coming back down the hall to the livingroom, complaining aloud.

"I called the store. They don't seem to know anything about that skimpy dress."

"Quick," Ralph urged Kinkie. "Back into the bedroom."

"Please," Eddie said, extending his arm to lead her back to the bedroom.

"With you, I'll go. You're a gentleman." Kinkie said, allowing Eddie to escort her.

Emma entered the room chewing on a sandwich.

Eddie re-entered the livingroom, closing the bedroom door behind him.

"Things are all so muddled up nowadays," Emma was saying. "Imagine not remembering they sent the dress here. I swear. Madame Zlatsky's right. The world needs a new awakening."

Ralph was not overly fond of Madame Zlatsky and her mystical mumblings. So he didn't respond. However Eddie was aware of Ralph's complaints about the medium and, in the spirit of fun, wanted to hear what Madame Zlatsky might have to do with Kinkie's dress.

"I've always had a soft spot in my heart for madams," Eddie said. "What is the latest word from the Other Side."

"Just this morning, at the séance, she called Ramaputra into the ashram from the Other Side," Emma explained.

"Ramaputra," Eddie echoed. "Is he a spirit?"

"Oh, yes, Eddie. He's been dead for over a hundred years."

"Poor chap bought the farm, did he?"

"He didn't have a farm, Eddie," Emma corrected. "Oh, no. He was a great guru in India many years ago. And he visits us at the ashram regularly."

"And what does he have to say?" Eddie asked, actually intrigued.

"He says the Mantra of Peace will soon be revealed to us."

"What is the Mantra of Peace?" Eddie asked, actually amused.

"The mantra is a series of Sanskrit words that will bring peace to earth when everyone in the world repeats them," Emma clarified. "The world will then enter the New Epoch, and the people at Chez Cerise won't act so weird, forgetting about the dress they sent."

Kinkie had had enough of being stuck at Ralph's house. She wanted to get rid of Ralph's loony old wife and came up with an idea. She wrapped herself up in one of the sheets, went to the bedroom door and flung it open.

"Eek!" Emma shrieked.

"Goddam!" Ralph exploded.

"Aha," Eddie exclaimed, fascinated by what Kinkie might be up to next.

"Down on your knees, Mortals," Kinkie demanded, in a fairly good imitation of an East Indian accent.

"I am Kamasutra, the great Indian guru who has come to reveal to you how to find the Mantra of Peace the world is waiting for."

"Oh, Kamasutra," Emma exclaimed, falling clunkily to her knees. "How wonderful. Get down on your knees, Ralphsie. You too, Eddie."

Down they all kneeled before Kinkie's sheet wrapped form.

"You, Madame, are to be the harbinger of the New Epoch," Kinkie announced to Emma.

"Isn't that wonderful?" Emma asked her kneeling companions.

They were unable to utter a word.

"What must I do, Kamasutra?" Emma pleaded.

"There is a Starbucks coffeehouse at Hollywood and McCadden," Kinkie explained. "You, Madame, must go there immediately, while the vibrations are right. When you get there, you will encounter a man wearing a hat."

"A hat," Emma agreed.

"That man will utter the Mantra of Peace," Kinkie elaborated. "Do not say a word to him. He is a spirit who is there only to bring the Mantra to the world, not to address mortals. When you hear the Mantra, it is being your task to be getting everyone you see from then on to be saying that same Mantra to usher in the New Epoch."

"Isn't that wonderful?" Emma enthused.

"But you must be going right now. Chop-chop!" Kinkie commanded. "The vibrations will not be waiting too long. Good bye, Madame."

Emma rushed to the door. "I'm coming, I'm coming," she shouted, and was out of the house in a trice.

Kinkie dropped the sheet, standing now before the Muskrats in all her splendid nudity.

"That was stupid," Ralph said.

"That was awesome," Eddie said.

"That was fun," Kinkie said.

Kinkie and Eddie laughed.

"Now," Kinkie advised. "You two darling boys go rustle me up something I can wear to get outta here. Nothing you find's gonna fit me. But maybe my dress is still around somewhere.Do the best you can."

That sounded like good advice to the Muskrats, and away they scurried to see what they could find.

Kinkie kept herself wrapped up in the sheet, and chuckled. It had been great fun being the dead guru. What fools most people are. They kept Kinkie constantly amused.

There was a knock at the door. Kinkie, wrapping her sheets back over her nudity, went to see who it was.

It was a gentleman wearing expensive Western garb who greeted her with a warm hug.

"I'm your Unkie Al from Madrazo, Arizona," the man standing in the doorway announced. "I never got a chance to meet you when Nephew Ralph and you got married. Holy Christ! He sure did pick a winner."

"Won't you come in, Unkie Al," Kinkie invited.

"You *are* a sight for sore eyes," Unkie said. "I always thought my sister's son was a dud. But now that I see you, I *do* believe he's a man after his Unkie's heart."

"You're a sweetheart, Unkie Al," Kinkie said, amused. She thought this was really fun.

Kinkie was always adventurous and interested in pushing the envelope. She let the sheet drop, apparently inadvertently, displaying her perfectly formed left breast. Unkie's eyes practically popped out of his head.

"You certainly are something else," he said.

"Thank you, Unkie. I've so wanted to meet you," Kinkie extemporized. "I love to meet Ralph's relatives. I think it's always nice to be nice to relatives, don't you?"

This time she uncovered the other breast. She left no doubt that the action was on purpose.

Unkie Al was a man of the world. He didn't miss a beat.

"Well, Dear," he said. "I want you to know, if you're nice to Unkie Al, Unkie Al will be nice to you."

He hesitated a moment.

"And, of course, to Ralph."

Kinkie was much less interested in what Unkie might do for Ralph. But she could tell that this was obviously a man of means. And he might be able to do very well by her.

"What brings you all the way from Arizona to Hollywood Unkie?" she asked, covering the bosom display provocatively and scrutinizing his fly.

Unkie Al decided positively that he was going to like his new-found niece very much.

"I came about Pansy," he said, making it clear that he was responding to her attentions to his crotch with enthusiasm.

"Pansy?"

"My ward," Unkie explained. "Didn't my nephew tell you about her? She's been a millstone around my neck since I was left with her. A niece. A poor niece. They're the worst kind."

"Absolutely," Kinkie agreed.

"I've got to get her married off. Can't have her on my hands forever, can I?"

"I should think not," Kinkie agreed.

"So I'm marrying her off to one of my other nephews. No blood relationship between the two."

"I can tell you're a very forward thinking man," Kinkie told him, pulling the sheet up to display a perfectly turned ankle. The action was not missed.

"The guy I'm marrying her off to? He's a financier right here in Hollywood. Maybe you've heard of him. Archibald Bumpkins?"

Kinkie had heard of Archibald Bumpkins, all right. She lived with him. Archibald was her boyfriend. But, as a Hollywood bookie and enforcer, he went by the name of Buzz Corrigan rather than Archibald Bumpkins. Kinkie was one of the few people in the State who knew his real name. And she was just now finding out that the rat was going to marry some broad from Madrazo, Arizona. Wherever that was.

"Oh, Archibald," she enthused. "He's real well known here in Hollywood. Going to marry Pansy, is he?"

"Yep. And what I came to California for was to make sure you and my nephew Ralph will be down in Madrazo this evening for the engagement party at Chupapollo Ranch. That's my estate over Arizona way."

That was a party Kinkie had no intention of missing. She'd be there all right. And see that that rat Buzz got what was coming to him. Two-timing her for some country girl. And if she could make out with her new-found Unkie Al, there might be something in it for a doting niece.

"What I was thinking," Unkie Al continued. "Was that I'd like you, being the right age and a relative and all, to be the matron of honor and the hostess at the engagement party. I wrote you a letter about it. Did you get it yet?"

"The mail's real slow around these parts, Unkie Al," Kinkie explained. "But of course Ralph and I will be there. We wouldn't miss the party for worlds."

Kinkie was tickled pink. And to show her gratitude, she nuzzled up to Unkie, gave him a kiss that was definitely not niece-like. As a matter of fact, it was graced by a gentle rub to the bulge in his pants.

Unkie kissed her back, with a tongue-thrust that showed expertise in the kissing realm. A hand went around her and caressed her lovely ass.

"Unkie Dear," she said. "When I get to Chupapollo, I have a very special present for you."

"Do tell me," Unkie urged

"Do you like music, Unkie?"

Unkie said he was very fond of...music.

"Mouth music is one of my specialties," she said.

Unkie understood. He had found his favorite niece.

Just then, Ralph entered the room with Kinkie's dress that Emma had left in her room.

"Here it is," he began. Then he stopped dead in his tracks. There was Unkie Al was in the living room talking to Kinkie. And the lapdancer was still clad in only a sheet and smiling sweetly at him.

"Unkie!" Ralph gasped. "What brings you here?"

"I was just telling your wife here about the big engagement party tomorrow at Chupapollo Ranch. I wrote you about it. Didn't you get my letter?"

Ralph didn't remember any letter. But then, with the postal service such as it is...

Whoa! Wait a minute here. Wife?

Ralph needed to explain Kinkie away. Unkie had never met Emma. But he couldn't let Unkie Al think this woman wrapped in a sheet was his wife.

"Unkie really wants us to be at the big party. And we wouldn't want to upset him by not going, would we Ralphie Dear?" Kinkie exclaimed.

Poor Ralph was flummoxed. He truly had no idea what to say. The situation was getting crazy. Unkie Al was his only hope of getting out from under Emma's heavy hand. He needed to be named as heir to the old gent. And Ralph could see that Unkie was quite taken with Kinkie.

"We'll be there, Unkie," Ralph said, not sure how he would manage to cope with this situation.

"I knew you wouldn't disappoint me, Nephew," Unkie said.

He reached into his coat pocket.

"Here are a couple of plane tickets I brought for you two. Jimsair flies from Burbank to Diamondback City Airport, charter flight. Catch the plane at four this afternoon, and I'll see you two are picked up at the airport and delivered to my ranch in Madrazo."

Ralph's heart buzzed. But, one way or another, he'd make this work. He had to make sure Unkie Al would be happy with his Nephew Ralph.

"I'll just go in the other room and change into something more decent than these old sheets," Kinkie said. And she disappeared into the other room.

Unkie Al gave his nephew a gentle punch on the arm.

"Quite a little gal you got yourself hitched to there, Ralph. I didn't know you had it in you. I'd somehow pegged you as a loser before, if you know what I mean. But now I see you have what it takes. Yes siree, Old Unkie's right proud of you. Real, real proud."

Eddie came sauntering into the livingroom, saying he couldn't find Kinkie's dress.

"Unkie Al," Ralph said. "This is my friend Eddie. I've known him for years."

Eddie was aware that Unkie was his friend's *rich* uncle. He liked rich people a lot.

Eddie and Unkie shook hands heartily.

"Uh, Unkie," Ralph said, apologetically. "Eddie just came here to give me an update on a friend's health. Guy we know who's in the hospital. Will you excuse us for just a moment while we go into the hallway for a brief conversation?"

Unkie was an understanding kind of guy. "Of course, Ralph. Circle of trust matter. No one else's business. Even dear relatives."

Ralph expressed his gratitude at his uncle's understanding and pulled Eddie into the hallway.

Ralph addressed Eddie urgently:

"Kinkie's in the bedroom there. I found her dress and she's putting it on."

"That's good."

"What's not good is that Unkie thinks Kinkie is Emma."

"So, tell him she's not," Eddie advised.

"I can't."

"Why not?" Eddie wondered.

"Because I think he'll disinherit me if I do," Ralph explained. "So you've just got to play along with me on this. The only way I can get free of

Emma is by inheriting Unkie's money. And Kinkie really impresses him. She's my ticket to freedom, Buddy. Freedom."

Eddie was amused by the situation. And would, of course, play along with his buddy.

"I don't know how you get yourself into these messes," Eddie chuckled. "But I'll back you up. Kinkie is Emma. And who is Emma, then?"

"I don't know. I'll think of something. But, one thing more."

"Yeah?"

"I've got to get away tonight. Unkie's having a party at his ranch in Arizona. When Emma gets back and you leave here, call me on your cellphone. I'll work out my alibi before you call. But I have to get a phone call while Emma's listening."

"I hope you know what you're doing, Chum," Eddie said.

"I sure as Hell hope so, too," his fellow Muskrat replied.

Ralph and Eddie went back into the living room to keep Unkie Al company.

CHAPTER THREE

Ralph, Eddie, and Unkie Al heard the front door open. Emma came flouncing in.

She greeted everyone with "Tutti Frutti Frappuccino."

Ralph, Eddie, and Unkie looked at each other in wonderment.

Ralph broke the silence by introducing Unkie Al, taking a chance that somehow the world would not cave in on him.

"Hello," Ralph greeted Emma. "This is my uncle, Unkie Al Pughworthy."

"Oh, Unkie," Emma replied. "I've heard so much about you. It's very nice to meet you."

Unkie wondered just who this woman was who felt it was very nice to meet him.

Emma scolded them all. "Now, I didn't hear you all say it. For world peace now, all together, after me, 'Tutti Frutti Frappuccino.'"

The three of them repeated the words half-heartedly and somewhat stunned about what this woman was all about.

Emma was pleased.

"You see. If everyone in the world will just say the Mantra, we'll have world peace and the clerks at Chez Cerise won't be so dingy," she explained.

Unkie asked, "Chez Cerise is dingy?"

"Oh, yes, Unkie," she replied. "You see, Kamasutra told me to go to Starbucks. The one at Hollywood Boulevard and McCadden. So, I trotted right down there. And a man wearing a hat came in and walked straight up to the barista."

Unkie was lost. What in the world was this dingbat talking about?

"And you know what he said?" she asked.

Eddie wanted to get this over with, and said, "I think I can guess what the man said."

"Tutti Frutti Frappuccino!" Emma exulted.

Unkie whispered to Ralph, "Who the Hell is this fruitcake?"

Ralph couldn't come up with an answer right away, and held his peace.

Ralph's only plan of action was to get his wife out of the room.

Kinkie was in the next room and would have changed into her dress by now. He had to get her out the door without Emma seeing her

"With all this running around you've been doing, you must be exhausted," he ventured.

"Well," she said. "Now that you mention it, it has been an overwhelming morning. Don't you think so? World Peace is about to burst forth."

"Awesome," Ralph answered. "Now, why don't you rest up so you'll be all fresh to spread the word?"

"If that's all right with Unkie," Emma said coyly.

"Yes, Lady. It's very much all right with me. Go!" Unkie urged.

"Then I'm off for my little nappie-poo," she announced.

And off she went to Ralph's delight and peace of mind. But before leaving, she faced the three of them and shouted, "Tutti Frutti Frappuccino."

They all responded, "Tutti Frutti Frappuccino."

Unkie looked at Eddie.

"Eddie," he said. "Your wife appears to be a bit preoccupied with someone called Kamasutra. Is she quite all right?"

Eddie was appalled.

"My wife?"

Unkie explained.

"It took me a while to figure out who the lady was. With all that tutti frutti business. But then, I'm sure you're used to that."

"You'd be surprised what I'm getting used to," was all Eddie could say.

"Interesting woman you're married to," Unkie continued.

"Thank you," Eddie replied, getting into the swing of what was happening.

Unkie Al whispered to Ralph, "Aren't you glad you didn't get stuck with a dotty old bag like that, Nephew?"

Ralph was struggling for an answer when Kinkie came into the room in her dress.

Unkie's eyes lit up.

Unkie took his leave.

"Well, I wish I could stay a little longer. But I'll see you two at Chupapollo this evening. And, nice to meet you, Eddie. Sorry about your wife and all."

Unkie left the house in good spirits.

Eddie asked Ralph, "Do I understand correctly? You two are going to Unkie's ranch in Arizona. Where about in Arizona?"

"Madrazo," Ralph told him. "That's where Chupapollo Ranch is."

"And he thinks you two are married?"

"Isn't that fun?" Kinkie enthused.

"Oh, boy," Eddie said to Ralph. "I see what you mean about me calling you on my cellphone. You have to get out of here some way without Emma knowing what's going on. You can count on me."

Kinkie told them, "I have to run along to my place and pack some bags. I've never been to Arizona before."

She breezed out the door in high spirits with Eddie right behind her.

Ralph sat down on the sofa with his head in his hands. It was all nearly too much for him. There was so much at stake. He had to keep Unkie Al on his good side. And he had to keep Emma from catching on, for fear of losing her money if the thing with Unkie messed up. It was a headache to top his headache.

Emma returned to the livingroom.

"I just couldn't get to sleep, Dear," she announced. "With world peace in the offing, and my part in it, it's just too, too exciting. Don't you think so?"

Ralph had to agree. It was all just too, too exciting.

The telephone rang.

"I'll get it," Ralph announced.

Ralph had thought out what he would say when his pal called him.

"Hello? Hello? Yes? Yes, this is Doctor Ralph Harlow. Oh? This evening. Well, yes. I am free. But are you sure there isn't someone else who could take care of it for you? Well, yes. Of course, I'd be honored. Yes, I'll be there this evening. Thank you."

He hung up.

"What was that all about, Honey Dear?" Emma asked in her most treakly manner.

"It's the Chiropractic College in Las Cruces, New Mexico. The national convention is meeting there. And the chief speaker Doctor William Bonapart was to speak on "Spinal Corrections for the Hispanic Population." Unfortunately, Doctor Bonapart just fell sick and can't make it. It's a subject I've written about in the Chiropractic Gazette, and they're asking me to fill in. To give the main address. It's quite an honor."

Emma fell for the story.

"Oh, Ralphsie. I'm so proud of you. Can you actually get to Las Cruces in time to address the meeting?"

"If you can pack my bags for me, I'm sure I can make it."

Off Emma ran to get her famous husband's suitcase packed.

Ralph sat down to massage his aching head again, when there was a knock at the door.

"Oh, no," he said to himself. "What next?"

He answered the door. He found a rather muscular man about his own age standing there.

"You gonna invite me in or not?" the man said.

"Who are you?"

"I'm your Cousin Buzz."

"My cousin?"

Without invitation, Buzz simply stepped into the livingroom.

"I didn't know I had a Cousin Buzz," Ralph had to admit.

"Yeah, you sure as Hell do have a Cousin Buzz. I'm him. And what I came here for was to beat you to a pulp."

"Beat me to a..."

Things weren't going too well for Ralph that day.

"But, that was before I found out," Buzz explained.

"You're not going to beat me to a..."

"Naw," Buzz said. "Last night at the club..."

"Club?" Ralph replied, not catching the drift.

"The Pussywillow Club."

"Oh, yes, the Pussywillow." Ralph thought he should have known. All his problems that day seemed to flow from his ill-advised visit to the club the previous evening.

"My girlfriend was lapdancing with you there. Like there was no tomorrow." Buzz informed Ralph.

Ralph suddenly realized that there was a link between this so-called cousin of his and Kinkie.

"I'm sorry," he said.

"Oh, don't be," Buzz informed him. "That's all right. That's what she does for a living. The more lap dances she does with the chumps, the more money she makes."

Ralph didn't like the sound of that word, "chumps." But thought he'd better let it ride.

Buzz continued.

"But then, when the club closed down, Kinkie wasn't there. So I asked around. I found out she'd left with a chump named Doctor Ralph Harlow."

"Oh," Ralph replied. "That chump."

"No offense," Buzz apologized. "But, then, I met with my Uncle Al."

"Unkie?" Ralph asked, thinking it was a pretty small world.

"Yeah, Unkie Al. He came to see me about tonight's party. And what do I find out?"

"What?"

"You an' me are cousins. Yeah! You're related to Unkie on his sister's side and me on his wife's side. That makes you and me..."

Ralph calculated. "Second cousins once removed?"

"Yeah. Somethin' like that. So, blood bein' thicker than water..."

"You're not going to beat me up?" Ralph hoped.

"Bingo. So I says to myself, says I, 'It's O.K by me we share Kinkie between us. Especially now. Since I'm gonna be married to this Pansy broad.'"

Ralph wanted to set his new-found cousin straight on that issue.

"'Share?' Oh, no! The last thing I want to share..."

"Look, Pal," Buzz explained. "There's no need to back off. What I came here for is to tell you no hard feelings. I can't see why, as cousins and all, we shouldn't both be able to fuck Kinkie. I wanted to relieve your mind. And I'll see you tonight at our uncle's ranch in Madrazo."

Ralph didn't know whether to feel relieved or worried. While he was trying to sort that out, Buzz said, "Gotta get goin'. I have a few collections to make. In my line of business, a few broken kneecaps are part of a day's work, if you know what I mean."

Ralph had to admit that he did not know. And was not particularly anxious to find out.

Buzz was out the door, and Ralph was free once again to hold his aching head in his hands. He sat on the couch and wondered whether he should rejoice or just die.

Emma came back into the room with his packed bags.

Ralph gave her the peck on the cheek that passed for a kiss in that household and lugging his suitcase got out the door.

After Ralph had left, Emma looked at the table near the front door where they kept the mail. There was a letter to her that she had not seen before. She read it.

"Dear Niece Emma. My ward Pansy Bunns is getting married. I realize this is short notice, but I would be honored if you would serve as hostess at the reception Saturday night. We are holding a barbecue and celebration party..."

"Goodness," Emma said aloud. "Saturday, night. That's tonight. I wonder why Unkie didn't say anything to me about it when he was here. No matter. It's going to be such fun. Too bad Ralphie will have to miss the party because of his nasty old meeting. I'll have to go get ready immediately. And I wonder what airline can get me there. I'll call the travel agency..."

Emma jotted a note for Ralph and left it on the coffee table. It told him about the party and the wedding and told him if he should get back in time to try to get to Madrazo for the festivities.

CHAPTER FOUR

Ralph and Kinkie got to the airport and then to Chupapollo Ranch in time for the party.

Unkie met Kinkie with enthusiasm when they got to the ranch and suggested a tour while Ralph got unpacked and rested.

She, of course, agreed.

"The first stop is the bunkhouse," he explained to her. "This isn't really a working ranch any more, so there won't be anyone there."

"I'd love to see it," Kinkie answered, getting Unkie's meaning right away. From the outside, the bunkhouse was the most nondescript building of the otherwise very upscale structures at Chupapollo Ranch. Unkie Al led Kinkie in and proudly showed her his pride and joy.

Instead of the primitive accommodations Arizona ranchers usually provide for their fieldhands, the room the two of them entered was elegantly furnished and featured three of the most elaborate antique beds in the entire Southwest. Kinkie loved beds, and was suitably impressed.

"Oh, Unkie," she enthused. "I love it! I just love it! Beds are my very favorite furniture in the whole world."

"I somehow thought you'd like it, Emma," he said proudly.

"I just hate my name, Unkie. Emma doesn't really suit me at all. So all my friends call me by my nickname."

"What's that, Little Lady?"

"My friends call me Kinkie."

"Can I be one of your friends?" he asked in high hopes.

"Let me show you," she replied.

Kinkie reached up and grabbed the back of Unkie's head. She pulled down, bringing his lips to engage with her own.

As Unkie began the kiss, Kinkie's tongue fluttered into his mouth. Their tongues tangled and ignited sparks that coursed through their bodies.

With his hand, he caressed the top of her head. The effect of the stubby hair of her head being felt simultaneously while engaging in tongue play at the oral level was an experience new and delightful to Unkie. It had been years since he had experienced anything really unique and unexpected in the realm of erotica.

Kinkie disengaged from the passionate kiss.

"Why don't we get comfortable?" she asked. "If you can step outta those pants and get rid of your shoes, socks, and shirt, I'd like to put this dress aside and try out one of those neat beds."

Unkie did not need a second invitation.

Standing side by side in their nudity, Kinkie led Unkie to a gold encrusted Louis XIII canopied bed. It was a genuine antique that had cost Unkie a small fortune. Kinkie didn't know Louis XIII from any other Louis. But she knew what she liked. And she *loved* that bed.

Unkie followed her lead with no resistance whatsoever.

Kinkie was an excellent judge of men. And she had pegged Unkie Al as a connoisseur of female pulchritude. She knew, of course, that on any pulchritude scale she was Grade A, Choice. She decided to let Unkie start out by feasting his eyes, hands, and tongue on her exquisite body. She stretched out on the Louis XIII bed, put her hands behind her head, and asked, "You like what you see, Unkie?"

"You bet I do, Kinkie."

"Then just help yourself. When you've explored the goods to your heart's desire, I'll give you that little gift I told you I'd bring to Chupapollo."

Unkie enjoyed few things more than exploring a body. And he believed Kinkie possessed the tastiest flesh he had ever encountered in a lifetime of devoted exploration. He wanted to take his time. His eyes saw her body as a gorgeous, glorious playground.

Kinkie was in no hurry, and settled back to enjoy the ride.

Unkie began by nuzzling her neck. Kinkie always responded to that positively.

Unkie was an experienced lover and pleasured her by caressing every inch of her body with butterfly kisses. The butterfly kisses were topped off by an act of love.

Kinkie and Unkie Al lay side by side, each one satisfied with the experience they had enjoyed thus far.

"Now, Unkie," Kinkie said teasingly. "Are you ready to receive the little present your favorite niece brought you all the way from Hollywood?"

Unkie Al was ready.

Unkie remained prone on the gilded canopy bed as Kinkie rose and propped herself on one elbow. The place to begin with Unkie Al, she decided was with the eyes.

She lowered her tongue to his eyes. He closed his lids while her warm soft tongue played gossamer circles around the lashes. Next, what? Ah, yes. Earlobes. Unkie had sensual earlobes. It is a wise girl who can recognize that erotic zone in the man gifted with sexually sensitive lobes. She nibbled at his earlobe and then licked it, swooping her tongue into his ear. It was an unexpectedly sensual sensation for this prince of love who had suddenly become her sensual uncle.

Unkie asked, "Is that the mouth music you mentioned to me back in Hollywood?"

"Do you like the tune?" Kinkie inquired.

"Yes, very much so. So far."

Kinkie told him, "The best is yet to come," Here's the grand finale."

The finale was a Kinkie special. While giving deep throat to Unkie's dick, she inserted a wet finger up into his asshole and gently massaged his prostate. Unkie had experienced exotic sex in many of the world's countries, but having that gland stimulated digitally while getting a deep, deep blowjob just about beat anything the old fellow had ever been treated to.

When Kinkie finished the finale, Unkie chuckled softly.

"What is it, Unkie Al?" she asked coyly .

"Do you remember what I told you back in Hollywood?"

She remembered, but wanted him to repeat it now.

"What?"

"If you're nice to Unkie, Unkie'll be nice to you."

"Oh, yes," she cooed. "I remember. And I must say, you've been *very* nice to me. I've never had a better time in my life."

That may have been an exaggeration, but a politic one.

"Would you fetch my trousers over there on the floor like a good little niece?" he asked.

"Of course, Unkie."

She got out of bed and brought him the pants.

"Reach into the front left pocket and see if you can't find something your favorite uncle brought along for you," Unkie invited.

She extracted a jewelry box from the pocket.

"Open it, Dear."

She opened the box and oohed and aahed.

It was a diamond and ruby bracelet.

Kinki haunted the jewelry shops on Rodeo Drive in Beverly Hills. The name of the jeweler, De Groton of Rodeo Drive, graced this box. And De Groten carries the most exclusive and expensive jewelry in Southern California. This bracelet, from this jeweler, she knew without reservation, had set Unkie Al back somewhat more than two thousand dollars.

"How can I ever thank you, Unkie? This is *so* generous."

"You already have thanked me, Kinkie" he told her.

They both laughed.

They got out of bed, dressed, and left the bunkhouse to return to the party at the ranchhouse.

Gertrude Tweetie, the doyen of Madrazo society, and Unkie Al's ward, Pansy Bunns, were the first guests to arrive at the ranchhouse. Pedro, Unkie's majordomo, had welcomed them on their arrival and assured them that Señor Pughworthy was attending to a guest but would be with them shortly. As one of Unkie's oldest friends, Gertrude made herself right at home.

When Unkie and Kinkie came back into the house from their tour of the bunkhouse, Unkie introduced Kinkie as Emma. But he informed the guests that her close friends and relatives called her by her nickname, Kinkie. So Kinkie would be known as Kinkie, not Emma, by those who were invited to the party.

"Why don't you two girls go over to the buffet table, get yourselves some punch, and get acquainted. The bride-to-be and the matron-of-honor need to get to know each other, eh?" Unkie Al suggested to Kinkie and Pansy.

The young ladies went to the table where Jesús, one of Unkie's houseboys served as bartender.

Gertrude was all atwitter.

"Imagine, Albert. Your lovely ward Pansy marrying little Archibald! Why, I remember him so well before the Bumpkins left Madrazo and moved to California. He was such a lively little lad."

Unkie chuckled.

"You'll be surprised to learn, Gertrude, that little Archibald goes by a nickname now. He prefers to be called Buzz."

"What is the world coming to?" Gertrude wondered.

Ralph came down from the guest room upstairs where he had unpacked and then taken a short nap.

"Come over here, Ralph," Unkie called out. "I'd like you to meet Mrs. Tweetie, my good friend and neighbor."

Ralph's parents had mentioned the Tweeties to him when they reminisced about the old days. His parents had suffered financial setbacks in those days and had left Madrazo for what they hoped would be more fertile fields to the West. Unfortunately, Papa had not done very well, and Ralph was raised as a member of the poorest clan of the family.

"So you are Ralph Harlow," Gertrude said. "It has been years since I've had any word of your dear parents. How are they?"

Ralph was about to answer when Gertrude's attention was diverted by the arrival of her son, Percy, at the Party. Pedro had just let him in.

Kinkie was always aware of her surroundings. She had seen Ralph enter the room. And the new arrival caught her eye as well. Kinkie had a nose for money. And this young man smelled like a million. Or perhaps more. Carrying their punch glasses with them, Kinkie and Pansy returned to the conversation group.

Gertrude made the introductions.

"Doctor and Mrs. Harlow. I'd like you to meet my son Percival. Percival, Mrs. Harlow will be the hostess at the party this evening and the matron of honor at the wedding."

Percy barely noticed Ralph. But he certainly did not miss a square inch of Kinkie.

"Percival is interested in visiting Hollywood next month," Gertrude said. "He enjoys the cinema so much and would like to visit the studios there. But, I'm a little concerned that one of those Hollywood gold diggers I hear so much about will lure him. He's a bit naïve, being raised out here in the desert."

Kinkie told her not to worry. "The gold diggers aren't really interested in men with less than a million dollars. They tend to be very greedy creatures."

"That makes me worry even more," Gertrude admitted. "Percy comes into the trust his dear departed daddy left for him next month. And that trust is worth several million."

"Don't you worry," Kinkie consoled. "When Percival gets to Hollywood, I'll take personal care of him and see he doesn't get taken in by any of those bad ladies."

Ralph could imagine.

Gertrude, however was relieved.

"Isn't that a relief, Percival? Mrs. Harlow will take care of you."

"It certainly is, Mama," he answered, his eyes lighting up. He got the vibrations that this knock-out of femininity might just show him exactly what he really wanted to see in California.

That satisfied Gertrude, and she was ready to move on to a new subject.

"Albert. I understand you've added a new variety to your famous cactus garden. Don't you have a new rare blue agave?"

"Certainly," Unkie replied. "Would you like to see it, Gertrude?"

Gertrude and Pansy were eager to go see the rare blue agave. Unkie urged Ralph to join him. Ralph was always set to do whatever Unkie thought was a good idea.

Kinkie begged off, saying she was feeling a bit faint. She indicated she was somewhat subject to the vapors.

Percy volunteered to remain behind to see that Mrs. Harlow was all right.

Kinkie and Percy were left in the house with only Pedro and Jesús.

"Are you all right, Mrs. Harlow?" Percy asked.

"I'm fine, Percy," Kinkie admitted. "I wanted to stay behind here with you so I could warn you about the Hollywood gold diggers. I didn't want to worry your mother and the others with the gory details. I need to tell you... privately."

"I'm listening, Mrs. Harlow."

"To begin with, cut the 'Mrs. Harlow' crap," Kinkie told the young man, "Call me Kinkie. All my friends do."

"And, would you consider me one of your friends?"

"Oh, Boy," she said. "You bet your sweet ass I would."

That broke the ice.

"Gee, that's great...Kinkie. Go ahead, then. I'm all ears."

"Not with them around," Kinkie said, indicting the two servants in the room. "I don't want to shock the servants. Let's talk privately."

Percy looked around, wondering where there might be any privacy. Kinkie knew just the place.

CHAPTER FIVE

As Kinkie led Percy to the bunkhouse, the full desert moon cast its romantic spell over Chupapollo Ranch. As the couple walked side by side, Kinkie kept her right hand firmly clasped to Percy's right buttock. He had never had that cheek held by a female hand. He figured it must be a California custom. He liked it.

As a matter of fact, Percy had never even walked with a girl hand-in-hand before. His mother had always protected him against the local girls. His father had died when Percy was three years old. Daddy had set up a multi-million dollar trust for his son, to be bestowed when Percy would reach his twentieth birthday. Since the existence of the trust was known locally, Mrs. Tweetie felt a maternal obligation to protect her son against unscrupulous girls who might corrupt his morals in order to worm their way into his good graces and lure him into marriage. So she mothered him. And smothered him.

Mrs. Harlow, Kinkie, was the first female who had laid a hand on the virgin posterior of the heir.

Reflected in the moonlight, the rickety appearing bunkhouse assumed a quaint, Western charm. Kinkie guided the young man through the door and into the splendor within.

"Now, Percy," she began. "I'll bet your mother has told you lots about gold diggers. She's warned you about those vamps in Hollywood. Hasn't she?"

Percy gulped. "Yes, Ma'am."

Kinkie corrected him. "That's 'Yes, Kinkie.'"

"Yes, Kinkie."

"That's better. But has she told you exactly what they might do to corrupt you?"

"No, Kinkie. I always wondered."

"Wonder no more, Dude.Your friend Kinkie's gonna show you. So you'll know what to guard against when you get to California next month."

She had Percy's undivided attention.

"The first thing to guard against is some vamp unbuttoning your shirt. Like this."

Kinkie slowly, methodically, unbuttoned each of the buttons on the young man's shirt as he stood there stupefied but intrigued.

She removed his shirt. And with one swift motion flipped his undershirt over his head. She folded the two items neatly and draped them over a Louis XII chair. (Or was it Louis XIV? Who cared?)

She commanded Percy. "Quick, Perce. Get off those shoes, socks, and pants and hop onto that bed over there."

Kinkie pointed to one of the beds that had not been graced by her recent romp with Unkie Al.

To the young man's credit, his reflexes were instantaneous. He was fully unclothed and lying on the bed nearly as fast as it took Kinkie to slip out of her shoes and dress and lie down beside him.

Kinkie proceeded to make up for at least part of the time Percy had been protected from sex up to that time. She taught him as much as could possibly taught in a half hour's time.

He needed no lessons on how to suck a sweet set of titties. That seemed to come naturally.

He quickly got over the shivering as Kinkie's light touch caressed his balls. His young prick responded gallantly.

As her lithe tongue slithered up and down the shaft of his peter, he came.

"Don't worry, Percy. You're young and full of vinegar. We'll rest while you play with my titties, and you'll be hard as a rock soon," she advised him.

She was certainly right.

When he was ready, she directed his prick into the garden of delights, and the young man spurted a lovely gob of jism into the receptive womb.

When Percy was quite spent, Kinky lay beside him.

"Now *that*," she counseled, "is what you want to beware of."

"Golly!" he said. "Those ladies sure have their wiles, don't they? I certainly do appreciate you teaching me about them."

"You still have a lot to learn," she said. "When you get to Hollywood, I'll teach you lots, lots more. But for now, go over to that wash basin and get your pecker washed off. We have to get back to the ranchhouse before we're missed."

CHAPTER SIX

Kinkie and Percy were sitting sedately on a sofa, sipping punch, when the others returned from their horticultural foray. Gertrude was all agog about Unkie's acquisition of the blue agave.

"How are you feeling now, Kinkie?" Unkie asked.

"Percival has been very helpful. He brought me a cup of punch and it cleared my vapors all away."

Everyone was relieved except Ralph. He was wary of what Kinkie may have been up to with Percy. But he had other worries that overshadowed that.

But an even greater worry suddenly enveloped him.

From the doorway a very familiar voice inundated the room.

"Tutti Frutti Frappuccino!"

Emma stood at the door, suitcase in hand.

"Oh my God! Emma!" Ralph realized. Could it possibly get worse than this?

"Oh my God!" Unkie exclaimed. "The crazy lady! How the Hell did *she* get here?"

"Come on, everyone," Emma chirped. "Let's all say 'tutti frutti frappuccino' and get World Peace under way."

Everyone stood there stupefied, not saying a word.

Emma stamped her foot and insisted.

"Come on, everyone. Kamasutra said that everyone needs to say it. Tutti Frutti Frappuccino?"

All present, including Pedro and Jesús, repeated the phrase.

Unkie said to Ralph, "I don't know how your friend's fruitcake wife got here. But *you* get rid of her."

"Do you have a key to the door of the guestroom I'm staying in up there?" Ralph asked.

"Yes," Unkie said, reaching into his pocket. He pulled out a keyring with about fifteen keys on it. He extracted one and gave it to Ralph.

"Good luck," he said.

Ralph needed a bit of good luck. Things were not going his way at all.

Ralph rushed over to Emma, ostensibly to greet her and help her with her suitcase.

"Oh, Ralphsie," she gushed. "I'm so happy to see you made it here for the party."

"Oh, yes," Ralph lied. "I got word about the party and knew you'd want me here to be with you. I got Doctor Oscowicz to deliver the speech tonight in Las Cruces so we could be together."

"I've had such a time," Emma replied. "Trying to get a plane here. I went to Burbank Airport and all they had available for anywhere near here at the time was an air taxi to Diamondback City. Terribly expensive. But then, I couldn't miss being the hostess here tonight, could I?"

"No," Ralph grumbled.

"So when I got to Diamondback City, I got a taxi out here. And here I am."

"You certainly are," Ralph had to admit.

Emma rushed over to hug Unkie Al while Ralph headed toward the stairs with the suitcase.

"Oh, Unkie," she gushed. "Aren't you glad I made it before most of your guests arrived? So I can be the hostess at your party?"

"Hostess!?" Unkie gasped.

But the gasp was wasted. Emma had already caught up with Ralph and accompanied him up the stairs.

When he got her to the room, Ralph said, "Now you just rest and then freshen up. The other guests won't be arriving for a while. You want to collect yourself after all you've gone through to get here."

"Oh, Ralphsie. You're such a dear," Emma gushed.

On that note Ralph left the room and locked his wife inside.

When he got back downstairs, another guest had arrived. It was his second cousin once removed, or some such relationship. In short, the groom, Archibald Bumpkins, a.k.a. Buzz Corrigan, the man who apparently broke kneecaps for a living.

Buzz was in deep conversation with Kinkie. Kinkie was holding a paper bag. Ralph thought it best not to intrude. A shrewd choice.

Buzz certainly did not expect to see his girlfriend Kinkie in Arizona at a party celebrating his betrothal to Pansy Bunns. Both he and Kinkie had some tall explaining to do.

When Kinkie caught sight of Buzz coming in the door, she had quickly gone to Jesús to ask him the way to the kitchen. He directed her.

In the kitchen, Rosario, the cook, was busy. Kinkie interrupted her, asking for a pair of kitchen scissors and a paper bag. Rosario did not ask questions. Señor Alberto's guests could get pretty much whatever they wanted, no explanations needed. Kinkie put the scissors into the bag and returned to the party with her acquisition.

Buzz made his rounds, first, greeting Unkie and Pansy, of course, and then talking to the people he remembered from his Madrazo days. He reserved Kinkie for last.

"What the Hell are *you* doing here, Babe?" Buzz growled.

"I don't have to ask *you*, you two-timer," Kinkie snapped."I know you're here to get engaged behind my back."

Buzz was aware of proprieties.

"We'd better not get into a fight here," he said. "It would be bad for my image as the dignified groom-to-be."

"Exactly what I was thinking," Kinkie replied.

She was ready for the confrontation ahead and knew just where to go and what to do.

"Come on, Buzz," she said. "There's a bunkhouse out back where we can get together and yell at each other without disturbing the party."

Kinkie led the way, paper bag in hand. Buzz didn't inquire about the bag, having other things on his mind.

When they got inside the bunkhouse, Buzz whistled.

"Quite a setup Unkie has here. The old man's still at it I guess."

"Don't change the subject," Kinkie said. "You've got some big explaining to do."

She placed her bag on a near-by table.

"I've got explaining to do? You're here with that chump doc. You've got some kind of scam going. And you're not gonna mess up my chance to marry rich. When I spill the beans about who you really are, Unkie'll run you outta town."

"Look, Buzz," Kinkie said sweetly. "I guess we both have some explaining to do. Why don't we just lie down in that lovely bed and discuss matters in a civilized way."

She knew Buzz could never refuse a little carnal amusement. She quickly whipped off her dress. Buzz was out of his clothes with the skill of a man who knows what he's doing when action is offered.

They faced each other, in the nudity they were accustomed to in each other's company.

Kinkie reached into the paper bag and removed the scissors with her right hand. She opened the scissors around Buzz' balls. It was the most menacing situation Buzz had ever faced. And in his business, he faced a number every day.

"What's up?" he asked.

"Look, you rat," she threatened. "You blow my deal here and I'll emasculate you. You know I would, don't you?"

Buzz knew his gal. Yes, she would.

"So what do you want?" he asked.

"Promise me you won't spill who I really am. Unkie thinks I'm Ralph's wife. You don't tell him otherwise. And I'll let you off marrying Pansy Bunns without even a fight. How about it?"

"Yes!"

"Yes, what?"

"Yes, I promise."

Buzz might be a scumbag, but he was one who never welched on his word. That made him a good bookie and a good enforcer. He always could be counted on. If he threatened a kneecap, there was never a retraction. No amount of pleading could save that kneecap. Because Buzz was a man of his word. A good honest crook.

Kinkie put the scissors back down on the table. Buzz pulled her to him and kissed her with the kind of deep kiss only he knew how to give.

"Baby," he said. "You're the only broad in the world with the guts to pull off a stunt like that on me."

"I've got that kinda balls, all right," she agreed.

"Ouch!" Buzz said, visualizing that unkindest cut of all.

Buzz made violent, primitive love to her on the bed. There was nothing suave, sophisticated, or nuanced in his primal passion.

Kinkie was fulfilled.

When they were both exhausted from the exertion, they lay side by side panting and sweating.

"Look, Babe," Buzz said. "I'd have to be nuts to marry Pansy. There's only one kind of life I can lead. And Pansy Bunns don't fit into it. I say, let's you and me get hitched."

"Buzz Corrigan," Kinkie yelled at him. "Are you proposing to me?"

"You bet I am, Kinkie. We're meant for each other."

Kinkie considered the situation. She was pretty sure she could land either Unkie or Percy and be financially secure. Or marry Buzz and have the kind of exciting life she really thought she relished. She made a hasty, mad decision.

"Buzz Corrigan, alias Archibald Bumpkins, or the other way around. You're a rat!"

"Right," he agreed.

"You're a rotten, no good bookie and a cold, vicious enforcer."

"Right."

"And you make love like a wildman."

"Right! So?"

"Of course I'll marry you. You big lug. But first, I have to let Unkie know. I'm gonna write him an explanation. He's been nice to me."

"And now he'll disinherit me." Buzz realized.

"You wouldn't get much, anyway. I figure Ralph is on the fast track there."

"Right. But even if it were otherwise, Babe, you're worth it," Buzz said, punctuating it with a kiss.

They looked around the bunkhouse for a pen and a piece of paper. In a desk in the corner Kinkie found paper, pen, and an envelope.

Kinkie wrote her letter, put it into the envelope, and sealed it.

Back at the ranchhouse, the doorbell rang. Pedro went to let in the newly arrived guest.

When Ralph looked over to see who had just entered, there was his old friend Eddie.

Although he hadn't invited him to the party, Unkie Al greeted him heartily.

"Boy," he said. "Am I ever glad to see you. Your wife got here before you. We've locked her into a bedroom upstairs. I hope you've come to haul her away."

Eddie got the picture immediately.

"Yeah," he said. "I'll work something out with Ralph here."

"You do that," Unkie said, satisfied that the problem with the fruitcake lady would soon be solved.

When Eddie got aside with Ralph he told him he'd figured out what a pickle Ralph was in, and as a good fellow Muskrat, he'd come to Madrazo to help him out.

The two agreed that Emma had to be spirited away, but how?

Just then, in through the front door stepped Emma.

"Tutti Frutti Frappuccino!" she cried out.

"Oh, my God, she escaped," Ralph and Unkie said together.

Emma breezed over to them.

"Oh, hi, Eddie. Nice to see you here."

Then to Unkie.

"The strangest thing happened. I was up in my room, and somehow the door got locked. Isn't that strange?"

"Strange," echoed the three men.

"But, after a while I figured out a solution. I tried the window, and it opened. There's a veranda outside, so I just climbed out onto it, came around to a flight of outside stairs, and here I am to hostess the party. Now where should I begin?"

CHAPTER SEVEN

On their way back to the ranchhouse, Kinkie and Buzz saw the taxi that had brought Eddie from Diamondback Junction to Madrazo. The driver apparently hoped that a fare would be coming from the house, thus avoiding having to deadhead back to Diamondback Junction. He was in luck. Buzz hastened to the cab and told the driver to wait for him. He would be right back.

Buzz and Kinkie returned to the group inside the house.

Kinkie gave Buzz the envelope.

Buzz and Kinkie approached Ralph.

"Hey, Chum," Buzz said.

Ralph wasn't sure whether the word just expressed was "chum" or "chump." No time to make an issue of it. He had his hands full with somehow getting Emma out of Madrazo.

"Yeah?" Ralph replied rather uncommitedly.

"I have a note here for Unkie. Be a sport and slip it to him for me."

"He's right over there," Ralph replied. "Why don't you give it to him yourself?"

"Come on," Buzz urged. "I'm asking you nicely. I'm doing a

disappearing act from this lousy party. I think my going away will pile up points for you with Unkie. You'd like that, wouldn't you?"

It didn't take any more persuasion than that. Ralph held out his hand and Buzz placed the letter in it.

Kinkie confided in him.

"Listen, Ralph. You'll be glad to know Buzz and I are taking a powder. Together. I'll be out of your life, and everything should get a lot simpler for you with me gone. I want to let you know, though, I really think you're cute. Sorry if I've made it hard for you. If you know what I mean. I'd love to kiss you goodbye, but the real Mrs. Harlow might not understand."

Ralph was relieved. And he really was frustrated. He realized that he would very much like to kiss Kinkie goodbye. And, deep down, he knew that despite the massive problems she had brought into his life, he would miss her vibrant spirit very, very much. But all he could bring himself to say was "Goodbye. And good luck."

It was a mere matter of minutes before Kinkie and Buzz were in the taxi and on their way to Diamondback Junction.

Ralph saw Unkie Al talking to Gertrude and Emma. He interrupted the conversation.

"Unkie. Buzz...Archibald...my cousin,.."

"Yes, yes, Ralph. Spit it out! What do you want to say?" Unkie urged.

"He gave me this note to give you."

"Note? Why would Archibald give you a note to...Damn! Don't just stand there. Give it to me. I can't imagine what this is all about."

Unkie tore the envelope open and read the note inside.

Gertrude, sensing that this development might be sensitive, stepped away as Unkie read. Emma was curious and stayed right next to Unkie.

"Hell's bells!" Unkie exploded. "Flown the coop! Your wife and my other nephew are eloping!"

Emma responded.

"No, no, Unkie. I'm right here."

"I'm not talking about you, Madame. I'm talking about his wife."

He said under his breath, "Damned woman. Nutty as ever."

Pedro came to address Unkie.

"Señor Alberto. A large contingent of the guests is just arriving at the door."

"Gertrude," Al called to Mrs. Tweetie. "We have an emergency here. Archibald has just developed a sudden severe case of appendicitis. He's off to

Diamondback Junction. And I'm going to go attend to him myself. Would you let the guests know the party's been cancelled.?"

"Certainly," the doyen replied.

"Oh," Emma chimed in. "As hostess, I'll take care of it."

Unkie decided to leave it up to Gertrude and the fruitcake to do whatever had to be done with the guests.

"Come on, Ralph," he said. "My Lincoln's right out there in the garage. We're going to follow that couple and set things straight."

"You go on alone, Unkie," Ralph declined. "I'll stay here if you don't mind."

"Stay here? It's your wife he's...Oh, to Hell with it. I'll go by myself."

In a burst of anger, Unkie was out the door and into his car to the amazement of the large group of guests just arriving for Madrazo's big event of the season.

Unkie was a demon on wheels when driving on the open desert road. As he pulled up to the small-town airport in Diamondback City, Kinkie and Buzz were just getting out of the cab.

On the drive from Madrazo to Diamondback Junction, Kinkie got to thinking. Thinking real hard.

Yes, Buzz was very attractive, physically. And he was exciting to be with. But was life with a bookie and a thug what she really wanted out of life? How about security? And money? Lots and lots of money.

She decided she had made a very foolish decision in the bunkhouse.

When she saw Unkie Al get out of the car that had been following the cab for the last quarter of a mile, she was relieved. It was not too late for a girl to make a decision that would keep her in diamonds, pearls, and the other good things in life forever more.

Kinkie and Buzz stood facing Unkie Al.

"Archibald," Unkie said. "I'm ashamed of you. Running off with the wife of a close relative."

Buzz was nearly always cool. Except when making love.

He replied calmly, "If Kinkie was Ralph Harlow's wife, which she ain't, she'd be the wife of my second cousin once removed. Unkie, you've been conned."

Unkie was taken aback. What in the world was *this* nephew saying? Had the world gone mad?

Unkie Al spoke directly to Kinkie.

"Is that true? What my scalawag nephew said? Are you or are you not the wife of my nephew, Ralph Harlow?"

"I've gotta tell you straight, Unkie.I'm not his wife and never was."

"And are you going to fly away from here to marry Archibald? Tell me the truth."

"I'd rather ride back to Chupapollo Ranch with you and explain it all on the way."

Buzz took everything in his stride.

"Is that the way it really is, Babe?"

"That's the way it really is," Kinkie asserted.

Buzz tipped his hat at his uncle and his ex-girlfriend.

"Nice seein' ya', Unkie. See ya' around, Babe."

"See ya' around, Buzz."

Buzz turned away, entered the terminal and out of Kinkie's life.

"Hop in the car, Little Lady," Unkie said. "I'm all ears to hear your story."

On the way back to the ranch, Kinkie told all. Starting with Ralph coming to the Pussywillow Club. The way she told it, she was infatuated with Unkie Al from the moment she met him. Love at first sight. So she just did everything she could to get to his wonderful ranch. She wanted to make love with him then. And knew all she ever wanted was to make sweet love with him for the rest of her life.

When they got back to Chupapollo Ranch, Unkie and Kinkie made a stop at the bunkhouse. Kinkie convinced Unkie Al, in very physical terms, that her love for him was undying.

Unkie and Kinkie entered the ranchhouse arm-in-arm. Ralph, Emma, Eddie, Pansy, Gertrude, and Percy were the only guests who remained.

"Let's all sit down," Unkie said. "It's time to clear a few things up."

All sat.

"First," Unkie explained, "I want you to know that Nephew Archibald had a miraculous recovery from his appendicitis attack."

"A miracle," Gertrude exclaimed.

"Second, we were playing a little game here. When I thought Ralph's wife, Emma, wasn't going to be able to make it in time to hostess the party, I asked my good friend Kinkie to pretend to be Mrs. Harlow so as not to confuse the guests."

Emma didn't quite get it. But, for once, she remained silent.

"And Archibald had a change of heart about the marriage, realizing Pansy-Dear is too fine a woman for a man with a past."

"A past. Tsk, tsk," both Emma and Gertrude sighed.

"Pansy is free to marry someone more upstanding and appropriate," Unkie told them.

"Someone who is not living with that horrid Hollywood crowd," Kinkie kicked in.

"Isn't it wonderful!" Gertrude cried out. "Now Pansy is free to marry Percival. And they can settle down here in Madrazo. Far from the sinful perils of Hollywood. You would like that, wouldn't you Percival?"

Percy reluctantly agreed, seeing his vision of the vamps of Hollywood fading from the screen.

"How do you feel abut that, Pansy?" Unkie asked.

Pansy, as it turned out, was thrilled to pieces. She had nurtured a crush on Percy Tweetie for years.

"Well," Unkie said, clearing his throat. "Then I think we'd better get over to the courthouse in Pokotomi come Monday morning and get licenses for the double wedding."

"What double wedding?" Ralph wondered. And the realization hit him. He would not be Unkie Al's heir after all. Unkie was marrying the lapdance queen of the Pussywillow Club.

Ralph began to wonder what adventures might be waiting in store for him and Eddie when they returned to California and attended future meetings of the Secret, Benevolent, Loyal Order of the Muskrat (SBLOM), which would, of course, forever be held at the Grand Lodge in Caborca Gardens.

ABOUT THE AUTHOR

Tim Desmondes was born and raised in Los Angeles. He and his family have had business and personal contact with many people involved in the motion picture business.

Tim currently lives with his wife in Southern California, but outside the Los Angeles/ Hollywood area.

Sex and Loathing in Hollywood is his first published, printed book.

www.ingramcontent.com/pod-product-compliance
Lightning Source LLC
Chambersburg PA
CBHW071215260626
47162CB00004B/1302